The Snowman

Stories

By George Ovitt

Blue Mustang Press
Boston, Massachusetts

First printing

ISBN: 978-1-935199-16-8
PUBLISHED BY BLUE MUSTANG PRESS
www.bluemustangpress.com
Boston, Massachusetts

Printed in the United States of America

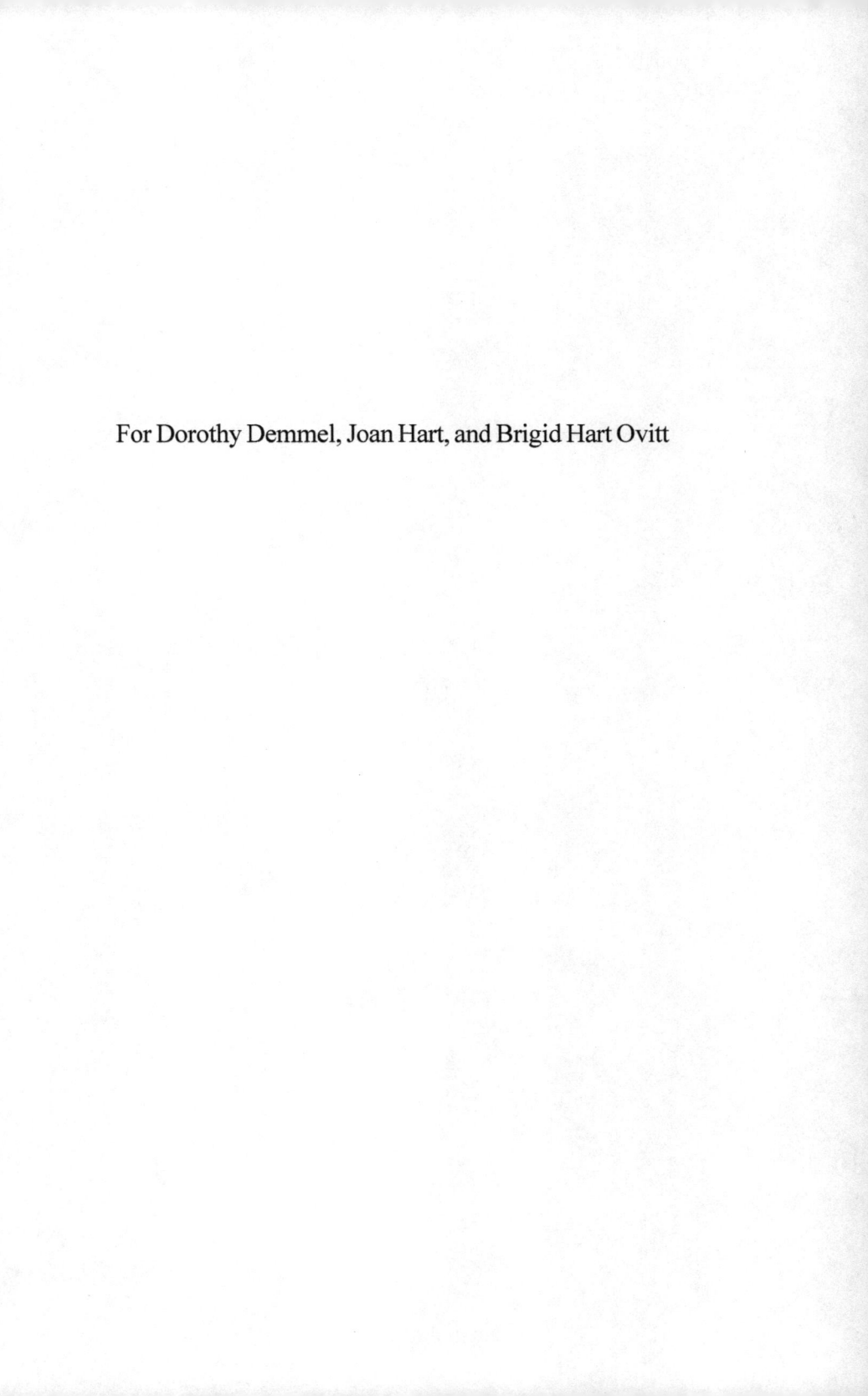

For Dorothy Demmel, Joan Hart, and Brigid Hart Ovitt

Acknowledgements

"The Last of the Dead" appeared in <u>Story Quarterly</u>
"Scene of the Crime" appeared in <u>Blue Lake Review</u>
"Axioms" appeared in <u>Oak Bend Review</u>

Thanks to the editors of these publications for permission to reprint.

The cover photograph is by Mike Ovitt, used with permission.

Contents

"I'm weary of every gasleak/Of abstraction."
Albert Goldbarth

The Last of the Dead

In the final months of the Vietnam War, in the late winter and spring of 1973, I was living in Browns Mills, New Jersey, near Ft. Dix. I had been processed back into the world during the previous year, but as a short-timer I didn't have any duties. I had been shot in the leg at Mu Doc nearly two years before, undergone a long rehabilitation, and now, after what had been a long night of the soul, my body was healing, or at least I thought so. The sniper round had ground through my hip bone, and the exit wound looked like the smile of a madman. My leg muscles had atrophied, making walking difficult. For a year depression had covered me like a cloak of darkness. I'd used Demerol and Percocet to ease the pain in my hip and had barely been able to endure my existence.

I was assigned to the base hospital at Ft. Dix for rehab, and since I didn't have any place else to go, I rented an apartment in Browns Mills and spent my days staring at the coffee-colored walls of my cheap room. I didn't know a soul. In those years Browns Mills was a small town. It might still be, I don't know, that part of my life is gone. There wasn't much to do but drink and watch television. I did both.

For a while I tried a job at a diner as a short-order cook, but I couldn't stand up for more than fifteen minutes at a time. The owner was a good guy, ex-Navy, but I was no use to him. He cut me loose after a week, with a bonus and a warm handshake. After a few weeks of sitting around watching quiz shows, the apartment began to close in on me. I found myself talking out loud to the TV and spending my disability check on bourbon—I could see that things were going from bad to worse. Then, just to get out, I took the bus to the base to drink coffee in the commissary. I'd sit there in the company of guys who were short timers, men who'd returned to the world, who were happy to be alive but who missed the rush of war, who were afraid of what would happen to them now that they were leaving the certainty of military life, and I would enjoy the sound of other people's voices, just for a little while, the reassuring talk about a piece of our past that was running away from us, receding into the distance like that last glimpse of Cam Ranh Bay as you were lifted over the South China Sea on your way home. But then they would ask me about my tours, where I'd been, partly out of curiosity but also in that swinging dick way that soldiers have of comparing horror stories, and it was no good, I didn't want to go back there again, at least not in the bluff way soldiers have of reliving their wars. So I quit going to the commissary and started going to the base library. It wasn't bad—no one ever went there— and I could sit in the quiet and flip through books of photographs and travel guides, dreaming about what I might do now that living was my only concern. After a week of staring at pictures of snow-covered New England barns and the alpine meadows of Colorado, wondering what it would be like to walk in a field of wildflowers but knowing that I'd never find out, I finally got around to doing what I should have done in the first place—volunteering at the base hospital.

The nurses were glad to have me. There weren't enough of them, and the hospital was full of wounded men, some who would recover and go home and a lot who wouldn't. I'd fallen in love with Army nurses when I was in Saigon and Manila. It was the same thing here. To watch them hover around those boys was heartbreaking. There was little you could do sometimes, but they did what they could, and nobody paid enough attention. Helping them made me feel like I had a reason to live. It was that simple.

In the early mornings, when the nighttime painkillers had worn off and the bed pans were full and a thousand bags of saline needed changing, I would go to the wards and sit with the men. I'd read to them, guys who had no hands to hold a book, or eyes with which to read. They liked magazines, stories about sports cars and fishing and hunting. If they were white they were country boys, mostly from the South; if they were black they were from the cities. It didn't matter. Every grunt likes to hear about cars and women, about dropping a line in the local pond or tracking deer. We were all the same underneath, black and white, crackers and city spades, just boys who'd been in the shit and gotten hurt, scared and alone, dying maybe, or already dead and just waiting around for the pine box and a hole under an oak tree back home.

I didn't hunt or fish or drive—I never had. They got me right out of high school, and there wasn't any time for me to have a hobby. But I could read, and the words and pictures seemed to calm them down, at least those who weren't beyond being calmed. Some of them didn't want me around, and that was fine too. They'd shake their heads or turn away or tell me to fuck off— couldn't I see they wanted to be left alone? And a few would ask me about my leg, and we might talk about the war, but not much. They were over it and didn't want to go back.

The surgical wards were dingy. Dim sunlight leaked through the dirty windows. The place needed paint and cleaning—there was a thick smell of disinfectant hanging in the air, but not thick enough to disguise the stench of urine and feces and sweat. It was quiet in some places and loud with complaint in others—it was hell. A chaplain once told me that God would look after me. I hoped he was right, but from what I've seen of Earth I doubt God pays much attention.

After a few days I started visiting with one man in particular, Henry Clevenger, a Staff Sergeant from Wilmington, North Carolina, who was recovering from the loss of his legs and from other injuries sustained in a mortar attack at An Loc. The battle for the provincial capital had taken place nearly a year earlier. Clevenger was leading a platoon of the 101st during the Easter Offensive when he was hit by shrapnel from an 81-mm round. He was medevac'd to a hospital in Saigon where his legs were amputated above the knees. In another war Clevenger would have died on the battlefield. I suppose you could say he was lucky to be alive. But he didn't say it and neither did I.

Did you ever think about that phrase, what it really means? Life is luck. Meaning that you can't count on it—it isn't a given. You're standing in the wrong place, just by a foot or two, or you turn you head at the wrong moment, or, like me, you don't run as fast as you should—maybe you're tired or carrying too much equipment, or your attention has wandered to home, to your girlfriend or mother—who can say? Clevenger was in the wrong place, but not as wrong a place as he might have been. I was jogging across a clearing a little too slowly. We were lucky, both of us were lucky.

Clevenger's father owned an auto repair shop in Wilmington, and Clevenger's dream had been to work there, to fix cars, maybe to race them—to marry and have kids. He said that he knew he wouldn't be doing any of these things now. Maybe before he lost his legs he'd never given a thought to being a father or a husband. It's like that. You only consider what you want when it's beyond your reach.

Clevenger said that he had survived ten months in combat imagining the pleasure of working on car engines. A lot of guys did that. I never did, not because I didn't believe in the future, but because I couldn't think of anything I wanted to do, or be, when I got home. After a few months I gave up trying to find a reason to stay alive. I just decided to let it go, and then being there was easier. I wanted to live, but not for any reason. Just living seemed good enough.

It had taken Clevenger months of rehab to begin to recover, but even as he learned how to stumble along on prosthetic legs, something worse began to go wrong inside of him. Like me, he'd slogged through jungle saturated with Agent Orange. We didn't know then what it would do to us. The brass told us it was harmless, not to worry. They were lying, of course. And now the war was in Clevenger's bones, and after months of hopeful recovery, he began to weaken, and to require hospitalization.

During the time he had been in the hospital or in therapy, he hadn't been back to North Carolina or seen his family. His mother was sick with cancer, and according to Clevenger his father didn't want to see him.

"He says it's too much strain for them to see me now, like this."

"Like what?"

"Fucked up. Legless. In this shithole. Take your pick."

"How's he know about this place?"

"I told him. He says it would be too hard on my mother."

"What are they waiting for?"

"He said they'd come when I was better. Like I've got the fucking flu."

"They mean well. Probably they're afraid. It's hard to take."

"I suppose."

"My mother's the same. My sister. They get nervous when I'm around."

"But you see them?"

"Not really. Once or twice. They look through me. I'm a ghost to them."

"Still, it's something. My parents call here on Sundays. Like I'm at college. My mother asks if I need anything. I want to say, 'yeah, legs,' but who could say that to their mother?"

"That's hard. I mean, the calls must be tough."

"Yeah. Fuck it. I don't care anymore."

I wasn't any help. My attempts to distract Clevenger went nowhere. Sometimes we sat in silence. I couldn't think of anything to say. He didn't want to talk but he didn't want me to go away. So we sat. Sometimes I'd rub his shoulders for him or massage what was left of his legs—they itched in the warming air, and Clevenger's eyes would tear up when I touched him. He'd look away and ask me to leave, or he would look right at me and say thank you. Or he would close his eyes and sleep, or pretend to sleep. You didn't want to think about what his dreams were like.

Weeks went by. The time I spent with Clevenger started to weigh on me. We sat in a silence filled with his sorrow and my yearning to ease it. I started to think about Clevenger all the time. About his being alone and the burden that had fallen to me. I wanted to save him. He was me in some way, or part of me. It's hard to describe what I mean, and when I think back on those days I still can't explain what I felt. It's like when you're in the presence of a person you know you won't forget, but still, as hard as you try, you can't concentrate, you can't take in the thing that's happening because life propels you forward into a kind of blank, a place where you exist without thinking or feeling. It was like that. Trying to focus on what was happening was no good. It took me too long to act, to do what I knew I had to do.

One of the nurses let me have Clevenger's home phone number. It was against the rules, but she didn't care. People think the Army is strict, and it is, but the people in it are like everyone else. Sometimes they surprise you. I waited a few days before I called, dreading it, but knowing there was no choice.

"Mr. Clevenger?"

"Speaking."

"My name is Gibbs. I'm calling about your son."

"Henry? Is he alright?"

He had a thick drawl. A smoker's voice.

"That depends. He's still alive but he isn't alright."

"What do you mean?"

"He needs to see you. He needs to see his family."

"Did he tell you to call us?"

"No. He'd be angry if he knew. But look, why don't you come? He's in bad shape. He needs you."

"Mr. Gibbs, I don't know you, are you a doctor?"

"No. I'm a volunteer at the hospital. That's all."

"Then I think you should leave us alone. You don't know what you are asking. My wife can't travel. She can't see her son like this. We need to wait until he's better. Then he can come home."

"Your son isn't going to get better."

"You don't know that. What right do you have to say that?"

"I'm sorry. I've seen it before. He needs you now."

"No. It's out of the question. I won't subject my wife to such a strain. He had no right. He wasn't supposed to get hurt. He was to stay back, away from the fighting. That was what he promised us. His legs are gone. How can I see my son without his legs?"

"He's your son."

"You don't have children."

"No."

"You can't understand how we feel."

"How do you feel? Never mind anyone else. What's going on inside of you?"

"How do I feel? I feel betrayed. My country took my boy. I wanted him to be a soldier. But not this. Those others do the fighting. Not us, not my boy."

"What are you talking about?"

"Nothing. Leave us alone, please. We'll come when we can. That's all I can say."

"When?"

Near the end, I came to Clevenger every afternoon with a copy of *Catch-22*, a book my mother had sent me. At first I hadn't been able to read it—it was long and hard to follow—but then I got caught up in the story, about bomber pilots in World War II, and because it seemed so real I read it over and over again. I decided to read the book to Clevenger as a way to pass the time, and as a way to help him forget his loneliness. He endured my reading, as I stumbled through passages that were terrifying, darkly funny and sometimes just dark. Clevenger said little during the month it took to get through the book. He didn't laugh and he didn't weep, as I had, a year before, reading the book in the hospital in Manila. His only emotion was indifference— much of the time his eyes were closed and for all I know he spent the afternoons asleep. It didn't matter. We both wanted time to pass, that much seemed clear. At the end of March, on a day so bright and clear that anything seemed possible, I came to the end:

"*Yossarian jumped. Nately's whore was hiding just outside the door. The knife came down, missing him by inches, and he took off.*"

Clevenger said, "Be nice to take off, just get out. How come you don't?"

"Where would I go?"

"Home."

"I don't have any home."

"That's too bad. You got to have a place."

"I did, but when I left for the war I left for good. I don't feel connected to anything."

"I want to go back."

"You will."

"Maybe. You could go someplace else. You walk all right. You're gonna keep getting disability when you're out. Go somewhere."

"Where?"

"I don't know, man. Fucking Tahiti. You lack imagination you know that?"

"Maybe so. But what difference does it make? I'm done travelling."

Clevenger laughed at this. "Yeah, me too."

We were quiet for a minute, and then he asked me a question I had hoped he wouldn't ask.

"What are you doing here?"

"What do you mean 'here'?"

"Here. With me. I don't get it."

"Got nothing else to do."

"That's no answer."

"No, it's not. But it's the only one I've got."

Clevenger looked at me. Then he asked me again, with his eyes, why I was sitting there with him day after day. I tried to ignore the question, but it was a fair one, and he deserved an answer.

"I'm not done with it yet, with the war. Coming back to the States didn't make any difference. Not like I thought it would. I'm still in it, and it's still in me. I want to be near it, and here is as close as I can get. You're part of it for me. I can't be with civilians and I can't be with the heroes."

"So I'm elected. Your piece of the war."

"Something like that. Not just the war. Everything that came before. If I leave, it's all gone."

Clevenger almost smiled. "I understand. There's no getting done with it. It isn't done with us either."

"Who knew? When I was in Basic I had a calendar in my locker. I'd cross off every day, the way you'd count the days until Christmas when you're a kid. Then in Nam I counted the days again. But after the first firefight I stopped. I got superstitious. Like it would curse me to look forward to the end of my tour. But I figured it would be over one day and I'd go back to my life. Then I was hit. It changed everything. It turned out I didn't have a life to return to."

"I did. I had a life to go back to, or I thought I did. I had big plans. Not now though. It's over for me. The past is gone. I got nothing. No legs, no family, no home. Can you dig it? I'm a dead man."

"Don't give up. You're young and strong."

Clevenger squinted at me. His face was yellow, sallow and waxy.

"Fuck that, man. My life is over. I'm hurt deep inside."

Clevenger pulled on the sheet and showed me the scars on his abdomen. He was caved in like someone whose bones had melted in a fire.

"What does the doctor say?"

"The doctor says shit. He comes around and looks at my chart and grunts and leaves."

"Still. They fix people up here. I got buddies who are doing fine. No legs some of them." This was a lie.

"Fucking war. Why'd you go?"

"Why? Same as you. I was drafted. In '68. After AIT my whole unit shipped out."

"Not me. I volunteered. I'm regular army."

"Volunteered? Jesus Christ. Why'd you do that? I never would have gone if I didn't have to."

"My old man thought I should. Told me war would make me a man. Made me half a man."

"I heard the same shit from my father."

"Why do you suppose they told us that? I mean, my father wasn't in the Army. He four-f'ed out of World War II. So why push it on me?"

"I don't know. My father was in it, big time. Big Red One. So it was kind of natural for me. Maybe your father was making up for something with you."

"I was his substitute."

"Something like that."

"Anyway, who cares? Listen, I appreciate you coming by. I enjoyed that story there. I'm not one for reading myself, but it passed the time."

"Yeah. It does. You want me to read another one?"

"Naw. I'll see you later. I got to rest."

I was there when he died. In the movies soldiers lie in their comrade's arms and mention how afraid they are, or how unafraid. Then their eyes close and their heads fall to one side. Usually these imagined deaths are dramatic, and if the dying occurs in the middle of a battle the world slows to a stop, as if war itself respected the last moments of the dying. I have seen men die, dozens, and this isn't how it happens. Men pass from the land of the living to the world of the dead in an instant, without the time or inclination to discuss how they feel about it. If they did have the time, it's likely they would scream or weep—stoicism is only found in movies.

Clevenger died the way a man should. He was lying in his bed, not looking around, not speaking, and then he was "gone" or "passed away." These phrases possess a certain truth. His eyes didn't close, his head didn't move. I saw it happen, by sheer chance I saw him disappear. As I had done with many other men, I closed his eyes—there is an unbearable sadness in empty human eyes, an obscene blankness—and then I called for the nurse.

Clevenger was buried in Arlington National Cemetery, back near the steep hills with the fresh graves dug during Vietnam. He has a nice clean white headstone with his name and rank, dates of birth and death, the campaigns he fought in, the fact that he won the Bronze Star. I can picture his father and mother, if they're still alive, driving up 95 and into Arlington, parking and walking among the thousands of identical graves to place flowers on their son's little patch of earth. Maybe Clevenger's old man felt better about his son after he was dead. Sometimes it works that way. It's easier to love a hero than a boy without legs, just like ideas seem to move us more than people. I don't know. But sometimes that's the way it works out.

I'm close to going there myself. It turns out that the war doesn't ever let you go; it pursues you every day of your life, right to the end. You don't forget anything. And in all the ways that matter you never return to the world. I'm there still, with Clevenger and the rest of them, ghosts in the land, rising above the jungle like the white fire that's eating me up, the fire that burned up our lives and the lives of our enemies. In a little while I will join them. And soon all of us who were in that place will be gone.

Or maybe I am the last. It's impossible to say. There's no one here anymore, no one within the sound of my voice. I think I am the last one left. I hope that I am.

Pioneers

Matthew and Clare couldn't afford the house they wanted—they never could afford the things they had their hearts set on—so they settled for a run-down twin on a short block on the wrong side of Mt. Airy. A quiet street, but they were on the corner, and the boulevard ran thick with trucks and commuters fourteen hours a day. That first summer, while Philadelphia baked in relentless heat and the garbage piled up in empty lots during the annual sanitation strike, Matthew took the trolley downtown to Ace Hardware and bought a cheap air conditioner, the first they had ever owned, as much to mask the traffic noise as to cool the tiny two-story house. Fifty-six thousand dollars, all of it mortgaged at twelve percent.

Clare was a teacher's aide in the public schools and Matthew was a graduate assistant in Penn's history department—they joked about being bridesmaids in the profession they had chosen but, more often than they would admit, now regretted. Matthew was even talking about going to law school, but Clare thought he should at least finish his degree; what difference would another year make? Another year of getting by is what she meant, and the truth was that Clare was worn out by her life, by the unruly children she worked with and by the filthy city. It would have been disloyal, she thought, to

27

say that law school was a good idea, that going home to New Mexico was her wish—to tell her husband that she was tired of the gloomy weather, fed up with the crime and the sense of rot that hung over the city like the sooty air. Clare had read about William Penn, about the Quakers who had founded this city of *philos*. They had believed in equality, in the spirit of God that resided in every human being. But her daily life suggested other truths; her encounters with her fellow citizens reminded her that a young woman with pale skin, a peaceful woman who professed a belief in "community and non-violence" (nowadays Clare recited her credo in ironic quotation marks) was a fool—underpaid, overworked, and disrespected. Clare had learned that if she failed to address the disengaged parents of her students in anything but a reverential tone she would be accused of racism, yet she felt herself to be an object of scorn at the poor neighborhood school where she worked. Matthew had suggested that she was too sensitive, that the long hours and difficult working conditions had distorted her sense of the importance of the work she did. Clare found these comments patronizing, but she didn't argue with her husband. What was the point?

The house was a nightmare. The roof leaked; there were cockroaches as thick as stones in the bathroom and kitchen, and a smell—Matthew thought it was a dead mouse—seeped from the walls of the living room in which they had set up their desks and bookcases.

"It isn't that bad really," said Clare as they spread towels on the floor to lap up the brown rainwater.

"I'll get up on the roof tomorrow with some tar," said Matthew, "and we can put out boric acid for the roaches and mice and whatever the hell is living in the basement."

The basement gave them both nightmares. It was a black hole, rank and fetid, full of rotting slices of pine and oak—a workshop for a coffin maker. It reminded Matthew of *Silence of the Lambs*. They agreed to bolt the door that led down the broken stairs and not give the cellar another thought.

"We've never had a basement before. What would we do with it?"

"We like going to the Laundromat. It would be gross to wash our clothes down there."

"We could have root cellar someday. Maybe."

"What's that? I mean, just what is a root cellar?"

"Where you store your tubers. Fungus."

"Yeah, well, not me. I'll keep my tubers up here."

They went on like that about everything. The closets were too small, the hardwood floors had been covered by rugs when they looked at the house; now they could see why—they were covered with stains and warped near the radiators. The windows didn't shut properly. The one nice feature was the newel post carved from cherry and filigreed with tiny flowery vines.

"I love the banister," was something Clare said every day, like a prayer to the god of ruined houses.

So they did their best, as they always had. They made the house livable, not quite cozy, but comfortable enough, a refuge from the hard world outside. The city was falling apart—not just the buildings, but the people themselves. The *idea* of the place was full of rot. It was 1984. Clare said often that Big Brother was in charge, not specifying exactly what she meant. Matthew kept telling her that he was "focused on his inner life."

"Meaning what?" Clare was scrubbing the black stains out of the sink with industrial cleanser. Her hair was tied up with a bandana. In one of Matthew's white V-necks she looked at once tough and delicate. She had thin arms and small breasts. Matthew loved the line of her neck and jaw, the way her ears stuck out from the tangle of curly black hair.

"I mean I don't want to worry too much about things. There's no point anymore. Nothing's going to change, at least nothing major. So I'm ignoring the news and politics and everything I can't control."

"You sound like a Buddhist. It's kind of sad to be thirty and a Buddhist."

"I'm not a Buddhist. I'm a realist."

Clare smiled at her husband and then frowned. "Don't go realist on me, okay Matthew? I think we agreed a long time ago to avoid that trap. It's just a cheap way to get along. We're not going to do that."

Matthew reached around his wife's waist, picked her up and set her on the linoleum counter. He put his forehead against hers. "No, we are not. But I want to be happy. That's what I want. And I'll let the world take care of itself. Okay?"

The people across the street, living in a house that had been renovated, re-stuccoed, re-roofed, and painted a cheerful blue, were the *pioneers* on the block. Matthew hated the word, the idea of *urban pioneering*, one of those sickeningly trendy *New York Times* style-page concepts that set his teeth on edge. To Clare, Matthew referred to Rodney and his partner James as Natty Bumpo and Chingachgook. Matthew disliked his neighbors because he thought them pretentious, but at the same time he felt that he had to respect the fact that they were gay men in a "committed relationship," as he put it, and therefore admirable, or at least entitled by their own marginal social status—this was Northeast Philadelphia after all, the bluest collar Catholic-ethnic enclave in the City—to hold the view that any white person moving into a predominantly black neighborhood was the moral equivalent of a European making his way among the savages.

"Maybe when they say they're pioneers they're referring to Willa Cather. You know, on the prairie," was Clare's thought.

"I don't think so. Look at the house. Does it call attention to itself? I mean, it's blue stucco for God's sake. Have you ever seen a powder blue house in this city? They're making a statement."

"What statement? Maybe they have bad taste."

"It's over the top. They're calling attention to themselves. To their *existence*. They're gentrifiers. 'Hey poor people, look at us,' that sort of thing. Hoping they can change the block."

"You're jealous. They have a nicer house than we do."

"Everybody does. And you're right. I am jealous."

Matthew and Clare had the misfortune of coming from middle-class, white, suburban, professional families. They didn't say they were the victims of misfortune, but if they were honest they would admit that they expended far too much energy being solicitous of people who despised them. They weren't well off, at least given their educations. They drove a beat-up Nissan sedan, shopped in the same crummy markets as everyone else—you couldn't get a fresh vegetable in this part of Philadelphia for six months of the year—stood in line for their medicine in the CVS with a lot of poor people, and took the requisite amount of shit from the city workers who failed to provide the services—police, fire, trash pickup—for which they paid exorbitant taxes. In other words, they were regular people, with one difference: they were white. Plenty of people were nice to them, but too many weren't, and Clare at least thought her being a white woman was part of the problem. Matthew wasn't so sure.

"It's hard living here. That's part of the deal; you have to take some lip. It's no big deal."

"It's more than that Matt. Sometimes I think they hate me at work. Like I can't do anything right. And I'm nice. I really am."

"Of course you are baby. You're always good to everyone. We might be too sensitive sometimes."

Clare didn't argue. She worked in a rough school. It was what she wanted to do. Matthew meanwhile was writing a dissertation on the developmental problems of El Salvador. He didn't face the same problems—he didn't get it.

Their neighbors Rodney and James were a complication in their lives as well. Not just their house, but their way of life. Matthew wouldn't admit this to Clare, but gay men made him uncomfortable. Gay men in stable relationships seemed easier to relate to, but then again he knew that in the eyes of the "population as a whole" (Clare's term) it was maybe worse for two men to act like they were married. Clare's younger sister was a lesbian, and promiscuous, and his vague connection to Priscilla seemed to Matt to entitle him to some insight into the gay lifestyle—if that was the word for it. But he had to admit that the thought of two men sharing ordinary domestic chores and sleeping in the same bed was vaguely disturbing, though he couldn't have said why. He and Clare weren't rubes, but somehow no amount of experience ever prepares you for the facts of life.

And "pioneers" was too much, as were the leather couches, the vacuum-tube stereo (with a preamplifier!) that James referred to as "state of the art," and the orchids that filled the indoor greenhouse—too much in Matthew's view.

"It's like a spread in *Architectural Digest*," he said to Clare after their first tour of their neighbors' house. "Two Thermador ranges and a Sub-Zero refrigerator. Not just the money spent, but the pretension of it. Who the hell has orchids?" The orchids upset Matthew. There were twenty-five species, soft violets and pale whites, with Latin names that Rodney had recited one after the other.

"I thought they were lovely," said Clare.

"Of course they are. But don't they offend you? Do you know what an orchid costs?"

"Who cares? Don't be a dope. If they want to spend money on flowers, that's their right. Someday we'll have a greenhouse too. How would that be?"

"I don't want a greenhouse. Just a roof that doesn't leak. And their bedroom. Did you see it? A water bed, black sheets? I mean, really Clare, it's creepy."

Clare laughed at her husband. He was prone to exaggerate and sensitive to class conflict—"jealous" was her thought, but he might have been upset by Rodney and James in a way that had nothing to do with their expensive tastes.

As it turned out, Matthew was happy to go back to their house for dinner. They had a wine cellar, and Rod—as Matthew and Clare were asked to call him—was an excellent cook. Matthew was judgmental, but he wasn't a prig.

"So what do you guys do for a living?" Matthew had been anxious to ask this question throughout dinner. He thought they must be lawyers, though he couldn't picture James downtown in a business suit.

"I produce music videos," said Rod. "Actually I work in New York. We used to live in Soho but the rents just got too high with all the Wall Street types moving in. Now I commute four days a week. We prefer Philadelphia. It's so authentic here, so down to earth."

"Music videos. That sounds so interesting." Clare didn't usually gush, but she had to make up for Matthew's clumsy attempts at civility.

"And James is a poet. Here, look at this." Rod pulled a thin paperback off one of the bookshelves and handed it to Matthew.

"*The Sea of Angels*," Matthew liked the title. Sure enough the author was James McEvoy, and the picture on the flap was the man seated here, albeit a younger version.

"You can keep it Matthew. I'll inscribe it to you."

James scribbled something on the first page and signed the book with a flourish. Matthew was touched and embarrassed; he wished he had something to offer.

"So you two are teachers. That's so noble. I thought about becoming a teacher myself," James touched Clare's arm as he said this, as if to make sure such a paragon of selflessness was real.

"We're not actually teachers yet," Clare admitted. "I'm just an aide and Matthew's getting his degree. But that's our plan, to teach."

"I hated high school. The teachers were okay, but the other kids…" Rod shook the memory away.

"I adored high school," cooed James. "Coo" seemed just right to Matthew—soft vowels elongated like the song of the mourning dove. James was from Mississippi.

"You *would* like it. Lots of boys to ogle," Rod wasn't smiling when he said this.

Clare was sensitive to conflict in any form. "Well, I didn't like it or dislike it. But teaching has lots of advantages. And Matthew isn't so much a teacher as a scholar. He's getting his Ph.D. in Latin American Studies."

"Wow, really? A doctor? That's impressive." Matthew suspected that Rod was making fun of him. Well, why not?

"This wine is wonderful," said Clare.

"Yes it is. I love these Hess cabernets. So full. Do you taste the blackberry Rodney?" James refilled his glass. Matthew was slightly drunk.

The wine, the food, the comfortable furniture—all of it was lovely, diverting somehow from their bland little wreck of a house and circumscribed lives. Clare didn't have any real friends at her job, and Matthew was tired of brie and burgundy parties where his fellow graduate students gossiped about their professors. Yet Matthew had the distinct feeling that he and Clare were objects of ironic disapproval to their neighbors. How drab they must have seemed to these well-dressed, sophisticated ex-Manhattanites. James, it turned out, had been all over the world.

"You've been to Crete? I've always wanted to see Knossos."

"Oh yes, it's majestic. And in '72 I hitchhiked to Kathmandu. That was a mind-blowing trip."

"Can you hitchhike to Kathmandu? I mean, are there roads there?" Matthew was skeptical. He wasn't quite sure of the geography, but he imagined a trackless wilderness someplace near India.

"Of course you can. I hitched a ride on a lorry from New Delhi. Then a bus. Oh, it's a long story."

Then James would tell it, piece by piece. Matthew wondered if James was cribbing from Marco Polo.

"And Greece. Well, that was fabulous. I fell in love with a wonderful young man."

"Please, James." Rod was turning red.

"But it's a wonderful story." Rod went into the kitchen to clean up. Matthew went with him to help.

"He can be a little too much sometimes," said Rod. "He gets going on his stories. Half of them made up, just so you know."

"That's okay. He tells them well. I admire his travels. Clare and I haven't done much travelling."

"That's too bad. Teachers get such a raw deal."

Matthew didn't respond to this comment. While he thought that it was true, he had complicated feelings about being honest with strangers.

After tidying up the kitchen, Matthew and Rod rejoined Clare and James in the living room. The couples sat close together on the black leather couch. There was more wine, homemade sorbet, anise cookies purchased from India Palace. A feast, prepared and served with an almost professional attention to detail (real china!). Matthew was appalled. Could this sort of thing be good for one? Eating raspberry sorbet and drinking twenty dollar bottles of wine?

"So, have you two met Lurch yet?" James asked this question with a flourish, as if embarking on a line of discussion that would revive the party.

"Lurch? I have no idea who you mean," replied Matthew.

"I'm surprised to hear that. Lurch is your next door neighbor. Quite a fellow."

"James is being witty," said Rod. "Lurch is DeWayne Williams. He's this *enormous* black person who lives next to you, that is, when he's not in jail."

Clare perked up. "Jail?"

"Yes, DeWayne has a habit of getting into trouble with the police."

"He beats people up," added James.

"True, he does. And other things. Steals cars. I don't know what all. When he's free he comes to live with Mother. James and I think he's probably crazy. Mrs. Schwartz down the block has lived here forever and claims that DeWayne has been lobotomized, but I don't believe it. Let's just say he's scary and leave it at that."

"That's not good. I didn't know that. Will he hurt us, I mean, should we be worried?" Clare was pale. Matthew was resigned. Why shouldn't they live next to a maniac?

"Well, we *all* should," said Rob. "He's home again. I saw him just today. Free for a while, so be aware is all. I don't think you have anything to worry about. His mother keeps him inside mostly. I mean, you almost never see him. But still."

Later that night Clare made Matthew go downstairs and check the doors and windows. He pretended to be put out, but he wasn't. They both felt differently about their house. There was a weight inside of it, a pressure pushing against the wall that they shared with their neighbor. Mrs. Williams. They hadn't even known the name of the nondescript black woman next door. She never spoke to them; they seldom saw her, though from time to time they would be in the kitchen and hear someone rattling around next door. The walls of North Philly twins were thin. You could hear your neighbor's toilet flush, the water rushing in the sinks. The house was a curse, vulnerable to attack—that was what Matthew was thinking as he went around the downstairs bolting the windows shut. He and Clare were under siege—that's what it felt like when you knew about the danger, when you gave it a name.

It was three days after their weekend dinner party that Matthew and Clare heard yelling from next door. They were sitting at dinner, watching "Hill Street Blues" on their tiny television. Their favorite show. "Thoughtful television" was how Clare described it. Matthew liked the Captain's girlfriend, a tough lawyer, raven-haired and sexy. He didn't mention this to Clare. Right at the end, when, as usual, Captain Furillo and his girlfriend were in bed— "What's her name again?" Matthew asked Clare, even though he knew it was Joyce Davenport—he always pretended that he wasn't interested enough to remember, and it was just at that ritual moment within a ritual moment that the howling began. Not yelling or screaming but an animal keening, a high-pitched wailing. Matthew bolted up from the couch.

"What the hell is that?"

"A dog?" Clare knew it wasn't a dog.

"It's next door."

"Him? Is it him?"

"I don't know." Matthew smiled. "It isn't Joyce Davenport."

The howling continued. Then some pounding on the wall echoed through their kitchen.

"Jesus. I'm going to call the police."

"Matt, don't. He'll know it was us. Don't call. Let it go." Clare turned up the TV just as the theme music cued up. "Let it go Matt."

Clare wasn't a flashy dresser. No one would have called her stylish, but she wasn't mousey either. Her hair was long enough to touch her waist, and she had green eyes—she thought it was her best feature. Matthew loved her looks, but he fell for her in graduate school because she was solid. By this Matthew meant that she could take care of him better than he could take care of himself. He was dreamy—at least that was his self-concept. He'd read about self-concepts someplace, in Maslow maybe, and began to think about himself in the third person. How did he come across to others? And how did he see himself in other's eyes? Clare didn't have a self-concept, or so Matthew thought. She just *was*. He admired this, and feared it—everyone is afraid of self-reliant people. So when Clare told Matthew to do something, to not call the police, to not investigate what soon became nightly howling and pounding from next door, he did as he was told. Clare was upset, frightened. But her experiences with young children persuaded her that being quiet often worked—silence deflected anger, soothed a troubled heart. She had no experience of madness and no deep insights into other people's suffering. She was empathetic—everyone said so—and standing apart from what was frightening usually did no harm. But she knew that if she and her husband were living a few feet away from a dangerous criminal they would have to do something at some point. She had no idea what, and there was no point in planning a response.

Weeks passed. Early autumn, with its lovely cool days, came and went. There was a respite from next door; it was quiet at night. Clare and Matthew put Lurch out of their minds. They went to work, ate meals, watched television, read their serious books. November arrived and with it the gloom that would reign over the city for the next six months. Then a storm ripped through the Northeast and dumped twenty-two inches of snow on Philadelphia—a record. Mountains of white filled streets that were never plowed. Clare had four days off from work. Matthew sat in the study, trying to work up some interest in his dissertation. No one seemed to mind that the city had come to a standstill—the Mayor appeared on television demanding federal disaster relief money—Matthew noticed that his street was plowed. Clare argued that the snow was a metaphor for the death of urban America, that the once dynamic *polis* had been immobilized by forces beyond human control.

"Think of Plato's Republic," she said, "the end of the City is stasis, everyone going about his business, no one allowed to change, the fascist Guardians enforcing a peace that kills the spirit."

Matthew liked the idea, but in his self-absorption he preferred that everything be a metaphor for his own ineptitude and isolation.

He said to Clare, "No, it's the frozen sea inside us. That's what it means. The problem is personal, not social."

Clare only nodded. It wasn't obvious what she thought about this kind of talk.

Rodney and James paid a private plowing company to clear the street in front of their house as well as their driveway and sidewalk. After two days stuck inside Matthew and Clare went for a long walk along the Schuylkill River. It was iced over and full of skaters, a cheery sight, like a scene from Thomas Eakins, especially when the sun appeared and illuminated the glassy black branches of the oaks along the bank. Matthew ventured out onto the rim of ice while Clare clapped her hands and cheered him on. His feet were wet, but he felt exhilarated by the cold, the sense of danger. On the way home they stopped at Gino's Tavern and had Old Fashioneds—it was the best day they could remember having had in months.

A day later Rod dropped a casserole over and told Matthew that he and James were going to New York for a few days, would they watch the house? Matthew and Clare were happy to do so; they spent two afternoons sprawled out on their neighbors' comfortable couches, listening to jazz and drinking Kona coffee. It struck them how much happier they were sitting in a nice warm house with a few amenities. But neither of them said so.

After a week the snow melted and Clare went back to work. Matthew took the bus to school but wasn't in the mood to do any research. Instead of working he spent a numbing progression of days in the audio center listening to music and watching videotapes of buddy movies that he had seen dozens of times before. He didn't understand why he was at such loose ends, and he felt guilty since Clare wasn't spending her days doing nothing. But each time he sat down to write he had the urge to have a drink.

A few days before Thanksgiving, Matthew roused himself from his stupor and went shopping. He would make a full-blown Thanksgiving dinner for Clare, maybe invite Rodney and James over if they were around. He picked up a small turkey and a couple of bottles of Beaujolais. Clare loved Thanksgiving—it was simple and domestic—and Matthew found that he was in the mood to indulge her fondness for traditions that for some reason no longer interested him.

As they were knocking around in their kitchen, slicing turnips and mashing potatoes, they heard someone screaming at the front of the house. Matthew looked out the window and saw a man punching a woman. Another woman was lying on the ground—she was the one who was screaming. The woman still on her feet was fighting back, but the man was large.

"Call the police," Matthew said, and he opened the door and ran outside.

He didn't yell out, and he would later wonder why he hadn't done so—it might have been enough. Instead he ran toward the man who was striking the standing woman while the woman on the ground continued to scream. Matthew felt blind rage. He was a coward, but at this moment he wasn't afraid. He flung himself with full force at DeWayne Williams—he knew it was DeWayne, and the rage that had been consuming him propelled his body into the source of the madness that he and Clare had endured for too long. He hit the man's back and knocked him down, but DeWayne was up at once, swinging at Matthew, not flailing but punching, like a fighter. He hit Matthew in the face, hard. Matthew felt something break in his mouth, and tried to cover his head, but he was pummeled in the stomach and kidneys. He heard Clare scream, then more yelling, then a siren, then nothing.

Matthew was in the hospital for two days. He had a concussion and a broken jaw, many abrasions, contusions, whatever. The first day, right after the incident, was a blur. He didn't remember anything about his encounter with DeWayne—the last thing he recalled was running out the door—the organism, it turns out, is considerate enough to shut down retroactively, right before an impetuous and self-destructive action leads to a foreordained trauma. Clare told Matthew that he had acted foolishly, and he had to agree. The two women whom Matthew had rescued had been treated for their injuries and released. They were grateful to Matthew, at least that's what Clare told him, but not grateful enough to drop in and say thank you in person.

"No one wants any help when you come down to it," was Clare's view.

And: "We should have called the police and stayed out of it."

"And watched those two get beaten? I don't think so Clare. You can't be a bystander. Remember that New York woman, what's her name?"

"Kitty Genovese."

"That one. It's not right to stand aside."

"I thought you were a Buddhist."

"Funny."

"No Matt, not funny. You've been in your shell for months now. So why break out of it in order to get beaten up? Explain that to me, please."

Matthew didn't have an answer, or didn't care to answer. He said he was too tired to talk.

Clare was both angry at her husband and touched by his folly, or courage, but she was also sickened by what she had seen. Though she didn't mention it while Matthew was in the hospital, she was ready to move—no more Philadelphia, no more urban life. It was madness to think a normal person could live in such a place.

The morning that Matthew was discharged a detective came to talk to him. The women weren't going to press charges. They were from Pittsburgh and had no intention of appearing in court in Philadelphia. DeWayne would walk away from an assault and battery charge unless Matthew testified against him. DeWayne would plead to a lesser charge and have his parole revoked, and since he had already been in counseling the judge would extend his probation or alter its terms—nothing much in other words, and nothing to keep him from beating up someone else.

"So it's up to you." Detective DiMarco was stocky and badly dressed. He didn't ask Matthew how he felt or what had happened; he didn't ask him anything except whether or not he would be willing to go to court.

"He's not going to testify," said Clare.

DiMarco nodded, as if in agreement. "I thought not."

"Wait a minute," said Matthew. "Why not? I didn't say I wouldn't." In fact he hadn't given any thought to facing DeWayne in court, nor had he thought about how he would go home to live next door to a crazy man. He hadn't thought much about anything beyond getting out of the airless hospital room.

"We'll talk about this later, Matthew." Clare took a tone with her husband—that was Matthew's thought. She was angry, he could see that. And so he merely asked the detective for his card.

"My card? There's an idea. Call me at the precinct—it's in the book," and he walked out of the room.

"You're not calling, Matthew, and you're not testifying. And, I may as well tell you this now, we're not staying in that house. I won't live next to that man. You didn't see what he did to you—I mean, you saw it, but not the way I did. And the women screaming. If it hadn't been for James and Rodney running over and yelling, and the luck of the police coming, he would have killed you. Do you understand that? He would have beaten you to death. I saw his face Matthew. He isn't...." Clare just shrugged, as if the word wouldn't come, or as if there was no word for what DeWayne was, or wasn't.

"What Clare? Not human? I don't think that's what you want to say is it? He's crazy, but there are plenty of people like him in this city. But not just in this city. Wherever we go there's going to be people like him. I don't have to go to court if you don't want me to, but I'm not leaving our house. What are we going to do? Live in a hotel? Move in with Rod and James? We can't just leave Clare. Think about it." It hurt to talk, and Matthew wasn't in the mood to explain himself. And he wasn't sure he believed what he was saying. But he didn't like the idea of giving up, or of being afraid.

Clare took Matthew home in a taxi. The house looked forlorn—Clare thought it was haunted by the malice that poisoned the city—something like that. Matthew agreed, but his impression was more concrete, more along the lines of how run down everything looked. If the sun had been out the last tenacious leaves on the sycamores might have distracted him from the cracked sidewalk, chipped paint, and brown grass. As it was, the block looked weighted down with sadness. He wasn't happy to be back.

Rodney and James came over with a basket of goodies, but Matthew hid out upstairs. He was in no mood for small talk. He felt broken, not physically, but in spirit. He didn't believe in souls exactly, and when he thought about his "spirit" he wasn't sure what he meant, but something like the part of the inner life that doesn't just fade away with time, the part that remains after the events of the day have been laid to rest. Getting hit in the face was bad, but worse was how angry he was—at DeWayne of course, but at Clare too, and even at his neighbors, who he supposed had saved his life. And most of all at himself for rushing into something he couldn't stop, and for being too poor to live in a good neighborhood—if there was one. His broken jaw seemed the reward for a misspent life.

A week after he came home, when he could talk normally and wasn't in pain, he took a bus to the suburbs, to Germantown, and bought a gun. He had to fill out some forms, and he couldn't take it with him—it was a chrome-plated Smith and Wesson .38 police special with a four-inch barrel. A couple of days later he went back, put the balance he owed on his credit card, and stuffed the weapon in his backpack. He also bought a box of shells, hollow points, which the salesman assured him had maximum stopping power. Matthew had never owned a gun, never handled one, never shot one, and had no idea what stopping power meant—well, the power to stop something of course—but shooting a person, shooting DeWayne, was unconnected to ballistics, gram load, caliber, and rapidity of fire. Bullets hitting flesh: now that was an abstraction, something like equity value or the Gross National Product. Matthew rode the bus home cradling his gun as if it were about to go off—it wasn't loaded, but that didn't matter. Guns were irrational entities, and he felt as if he had crossed some kind of line, that he had gone crazy, or would. When he bought the gun the salesman looked at Matthew's ruined face and said that it was probably a good idea to have some protection. Matthew was too embarrassed to say anything, but he felt creepy, as if he were buying pornography—some things are unspeakable.

He didn't load it. At home he pried open the cellar door and put it on a joist, out of sight. The bullets he put upstairs, as if they might load themselves and kill someone. Matthew understood that an unloaded gun was just a club, but he couldn't bring himself to turn the hideous piece of metal into a weapon. Despite its uselessness, Matthew felt relieved. There was something about it, about the commitment that it took to buy it, about its heft and lack of ambiguity that lifted a burden from his soul. Smith and Wesson sounded like a high-powered law firm—something to protect him and Clare. He wouldn't shoot DeWayne or anyone else, but he wouldn't be scared away. He didn't tell Clare he had a gun—how could he?—but the mere fact that he had done something so momentous without discussing it with his wife—in whom he had, until now, confided everything, and without whose sanction he would never have ventured to buy a pair of shoes—made the deception irrelevant. He was going his own way—he was doing what he had to do. He spent some time justifying what was clearly an impetuous act and all he could come up with was the conviction that people like him and like Clare were always being pushed around, were always on the receiving end of rudeness and fraud and violence. It had to stop. All the bad guys had guns; why shouldn't he have one? In modern America, a .38 was a little like money in the bank. Who knew when the shit would hit the fan?

Clare thought her husband was depressed. She was at work a lot, trying to make up missed school days, getting her kids ready for the achievement tests that most of them would fail. When she dragged herself into the house—not without a furtive look next door—she didn't feel like chatting. She'd pour a glass of wine and put on the television, "space out" was her word for it, maybe catch a nap before Matthew fixed dinner. The weather was still drab though not as cold, the clouds were as thick as ever, making Clare wonder if the sun would return, but with the shades drawn the world outside gradually faded away. Matthew wasn't working. He'd taken a medical leave. He was home, but he and his wife hardly spoke. Clare would ask her husband about his day and he'd be noncommittal, claiming that he'd felt poorly, his face still ached, he couldn't concentrate. He looked better to Clare, his face was healing, but he'd lost weight—both in pounds and in being. He seemed insubstantial, as if he might be blown away by the winter winds.

The moaning started again. Howling was more like it, a mournful cry, as if DeWayne was lifting his soul up to God or invoking Satan. Clare's nerves, raw since the beatings, were flayed by the persistence of the sound—it started in the evening and went on for hours, it echoed against the thin walls of the twin. Matthew put on the stereo as loud as he could bear it, but it was no good. Just knowing that a strange, violent human being was a few feet away made them jumpy.

"It's like he's calling out to us," said Matthew.

"A Siren. Was that it? They led sailors to their deaths."

"But theirs was beautiful music. This is the sound of death."

"He's quite mad," Clare was sure of it. It made her feel better to say so.

"Yes, he is mad. And we're here. What do you want to do?"

"I don't know. I can't stand this anymore though. I have to get away from here."

"From?"

"Here. This house, this block, this city. Matthew, we have to leave. I can't endure living with this fear."

"We can't leave Clare. We don't have any money. No jobs except here, and I don't have a degree yet. We're stuck."

"Matthew, I didn't tell you before, but I'm taking a leave of absence."

"What do you mean? You quit?"

"No, but I suppose I did. The principal didn't like it. She doesn't have to take me back."

"So how are we going to live?"

"I don't know, but I told you I can't stay here. We can go to my parents."

"No thanks. I'm done living with parents. Yours are fine, but we're on our own. We can't just crawl home when things get tough."

"Listen. Do you hear what's going on next door? I'm leaving. We can put the house on the market. Find jobs in New Mexico, or move to Denver. Anyplace but here."

Matthew was too upset to say anything. He shook his head and went upstairs. It was quiet next door, but that didn't matter. Whatever the world looked like on the other side of the wall wasn't going to change. DeWayne wasn't real anymore. If he moved out or went to jail the house would still feel haunted.

In the middle of the night, with Clare asleep, Matthew went to the closet and found his box of shells. He retrieved the gun and loaded it. He wasn't sure what he would do. Maybe Clare would leave him, go home to New Mexico or move to another city. He held the gun, felt the heavy steel, weighted now with six hollow points, as real as anything could be, an object, Matthew understood, that captured all of the madness of the world. Intelligence suborned by violence. He sat in his living room, the endless bad news on CNN spinning through the freezing night, a reporter at another massacre in El Salvador, the sound low, his wife asleep, or awake, or packing—he couldn't tell, didn't care—Matthew was waiting for something to happen, waiting to see what he would do to save himself.

The Egg Man

As senior waitress, Kay got the front dining room, the one with the new booths and fresh carpet. Ray the egg man called her 'Queen Bee' because of her hairdo, but not to her face. The other waitresses deferred to Kay when it came to scheduling and the division of tips, took to heart her advice on matters of service, and asked politely before they went out back for a smoke. The boss, Mr. Fernandez, only came upstairs after the morning rush was over, but on Sundays, when families dressed for church filled the tiny foyer and spilled out onto the sidewalk, Mr. F would pop into the kitchen and take the Wheel—the carousel on which individual orders were placed—pushing Bob onto meats and Mel off the grill altogether. Bob was the second best short-order cook I'd ever met, and you could tell that Mr. F's clumsy handling of the Wheel set Bob's teeth on edge. It was chaos back there on Sundays, 6 a.m. to noon, and my first day on the job Kay told me never, under any circumstances, should a busboy go anywhere in the kitchen except to the dishwashing station.

Me and Richie Ratelli were the top busboys and got the weekend shifts, six to six, when the tips were best. Richie had two years in when I started, so I got the back room, the one with fewer tables and newer waitresses. Richie was from Bradley Beach, a tough kid who loved to fight and would later join the Marines, and, later still, when I was barely out of high school, would get shot at Khe Sanh. But back then Richie was probably the best busboy in Asbury Park. He could clear a four-top in thirty seconds, a booth in fifteen. The trick that he taught me was sequence. First you scoop up all the silverware and drop it, quietly, into the top tray on the bus cart. Then stack the big plates, thick with egg yolks and fake maple syrup, into the middle tray. Next the coffee cups, tucked in with the dishes, cups tipped over and stacked. Glasses of juice and water go in the bottom tray on the cart, but first you dump the water in with the plates so it wouldn't spill all over your black pants and red vest when you're hustling to unload. Trash goes in the side tray, then you have to thoroughly wipe the table and chairs with a towel that's wet enough to get the syrup off but not so wet that the customers get their clothes damp. You have to change the rag after every four tables or you just smear muck on the Formica, and if you do that the placemats stick to the table and the waitresses let you have it. We'd work non-stop for six hours, one table after another, and if you had to go to the bathroom you'd be behind for the whole morning. I learned not to eat or drink for hours at a time, so after a week Kay took me aside and told me she'd had her doubts when Mr. Fernandez hired me because I was so young, fifteen I was that first winter, but the girls thought I'd do just fine.

It's the little things that make a difference Kay told me, like keeping the waitress stations stocked with napkins and making fresh coffee and running to the storeroom for tea bags and sugar packets and the dozen other things that customers want. I learned from Richie about filling water glasses and putting them on a tray so the waitresses could save some time. I got ten percent of the total tips, Richie got fifteen, but Richie said the girls would look after us if we looked after them, meaning you'd get your full share and not get stiffed. I never did get stiffed, at least not that I know of, and was treated well by everyone, that is by all the workers, the waitresses and cooks and dishwashers. It sounds odd to admit, but it's true, that it was from this crappy job that I learned how to work and how to get along with people.

Ray Johnson, the egg man, the best short-order cook I ever saw in my fifteen years of restaurant work, had been with Perkins from the beginning, starting out in Ohio in 1959. When he got out of the Army he moved to Asbury Park and took up right where he'd left off—running the fry corner like the King of Eggs that he was. Ray could prep fifteen orders, from poached to Westerns, without missing a beat, all the while listening to his little transistor pump out R&B hits, at least when Mr. F wasn't around to complain. Ray didn't like Mr. Fernandez and the feeling was mutual. All the kitchen guys were black and all of them except Ray acted polite around the boss. But Ray thought Fernandez was a fool and didn't belong running a Perkins Pancake House. For one thing, it was Ray who figured out that the boss was screwing the good-looking hostess who called herself Misty, and that was why a girl who couldn't even keep track of the menus had a job at the busiest egg house on the Shore. Ray had seen them making out in the basement office, but he kept it to himself until Fernandez got on his case about the radio.

"Least I ain't passing the time screwing around," was what Ray said, right to the boss's face, in front of Bob and Ellis the dishwasher. I heard from Kay that Fernandez just about fired Ray but that he knew better—the place wouldn't run without Ray or Bob as they did all the prep and cooking and clean up between them, and they didn't steal anything like Mel did, and the part-time guys came and went with their binges and weren't of any use. Truth was, even on Easter Sunday, when the lines didn't let up for twelve hours straight, and when everybody worked—four busboys and twelve waitresses—Ray and Bob could still push out all the orders without any help, as long as Ellis could keep the dishes coming and me or Richie could jump onto the line to restock eggs and pancake mixes. So Fernandez let it go, and so did Ray, though his radio never went off again. At least not for a while.

Misty was tall and good looking and stacked. She made Ray giddy when she'd flash a smile at him and ask for a white omelet. She had nice clothes supplied by Mr. F and wore sweet-smelling perfume and high heels that accentuated her slender legs. She had Mr. F wrapped around her finger. He'd climb with some difficulty out of his Coup de Ville, a muscular man gone to fat, a vain man who pomaded his thick gray mane of hair and wore a jewel on his pinky. He said he'd played professional football, but Ray thought that was bullshit. Anyway, he'd come into the House with a Macy's box under his arm and after a little while Misty would nod to everyone like we'd miss her help and head downstairs for her bonus—dresses and shoes and bracelets, and you didn't want to think what else. Ray said the sex must have been pretty good 'cause the payoff was excellent. I was a kid then and would have thought more about Mr. F and Misty having sex just under my feet but I didn't have any idea what to think. Sex was a mystery to me back then, like most everything else. I suppose I was jealous of the old man because like every other male who worked at Perkins I had crush on her. She came into my dreams sometimes, and I'd watch her out of the corner of my eye while I was clearing tables. But Misty was dumb, and she never had a good word for the busboys, and never lifted a finger to wipe a table as she was afraid to break one of her ruby-red nails or to get syrup on her nice clothes.

Six months after I'd started at Perkins, working weekends and two nights a week, Kay whispered to me that Mrs. Fernandez had caught her husband at the Shore Motel with Misty. How did she know that? Ray found out somehow. I brought up Misty with Ray on our smoke break in an indirect way, asking him what he thought of her hostessing skills. Ray laughed in the deep phlegmy way that he had, a good laugh, full of mirth and no ill will, and he said Misty was too dumb to carry a menu to a table and anyway she was not long for Perkin's since Mr. F's old lady knew he was screwing her every afternoon including Sunday at the Shore Motel, which fact he, Ray, had heard from a buddy of his who worked the desk at the motel, a hot pillow joint just across the street, right where Mrs. F could see the big silver Caddy parked all by itself in the middle of the day when she was coming home from Shore Lanes where she bowled three times a week in the Ladies Auxiliary League on a team called, for reasons that escaped Ray, "The Corsages." How he knew all this was a mystery. He worked twelve hours, six days a week, and lived way the hell out in Freehold, but when he wasn't making perfect eggs he liked to shoot the breeze with whoever was around, including with me, a dumb white high-school kid who was saving thirty bucks a week to buy a car.

"He's dead meat, so's Misty. You see Fernandez's old lady? She looks like a steamfitter. She'll rip Misty a new asshole, her." Another big laugh followed by a racking cough. Ray the Egg Man had grown up in New Orleans, and when he laughed, which was often, he sounded like Louis Armstrong, phlegmatic and sweetly harsh, Satchamo, whose hit song was all over the place that year. Ray smoked like a chimney when he could, and he'd always give me a Kool, which is why I started on the damn things, forty years ago now, but that's another story.

Bob would come out while we were talking and smoking and light up a Newport and say nothing. He was the flip side of Ray. Bob was tall and lean where Ray was squat; quiet where Ray was gabby. Bob's hair shone with gel, and he had the longest fingers I'd ever seen on a person. You wanted

Bob to like you—he was steady in a way I wanted to be back then, no frills, never a wasted movement prepping the batters or running the gritty stones across the grill until it shone. He never paid me any mind. He'd nod to Ray and smoke, doze maybe if there were a little sun. Richie said Ray had been in Korea when he was a kid, a POW, and he'd gotten fucked up in the cold, seen things, and that was why he was quiet and loved the sun and the hot steaming kitchen. Richie didn't think much of Ray or Bob, he didn't care for black people at all, though he thought Ellis was okay, weak in the head, but the good kind of black, not like the Negroes in Bradley Beach he and his buddies fought every chance they got. You could tell Richie was that crazy kind of white kid, angry and violent, but he did teach me to fight, out back behind the dumpster. He taught me how to hold my hands up in front of my face and pull my elbows into my body, how to jab and feint, and move my feet sideways so I wouldn't be hit squarely. He showed me how to twist my body into a punch and told me never to hit someone in the mouth or jaw—you'd break your hand—but to aim for the soft tissue of the nose and throat, "One fucking smack in the windpipe and it's over man," and he was right, as I would find out a few years later when, in basic training, a redneck from Huntsville called me out and took a wild swing over my head and I ducked like Richie had shown me and popped him with a short left hand in the throat and that was all she wrote.

So we'd smoke and talk, or not talk, and box and spit and curse and speculate on how Misty might look with her clothes off—good, we decided—and I was fifteen or sixteen years old, a punk, saving up for the Buick Skylark that I wrecked one black summer night on Route 301 outside Petersburg, Virginia, but that too is another story.

The thing about working in an egg joint as opposed to an upscale place is the way time passes. Later on, hoping to make more money, I started bussing downtown at the Berkeley-Carteret, a white-tablecloth kind of place where the waiters (no waitresses) called me "son" and doled out whatever few dollars from their tips they felt like giving me, no rhyme or reason to it. And time dragged something awful there, people sitting for two hours over their prime ribs and Merlots, whereas at Perkins you never stopped working except for the thirty minutes you got to eat and smoke. And the fast pace made us work together, like people did on assembly lines—I know, since I worked on one at the Rheingold Beer brewery in Newark—and we each had a job to do and everyone depended on everyone else. Ray could out-cook any one of the Berkeley chefs, whatever the food. He could make a roux with black-eyed peas and hominy and what he called "soft knuckles" of chicken and pork, greens with ham hocks, and the best barbeque sauce I ever tasted. He wasn't just about eggs. But Ray never bragged. And Ellis, about eighty years old, with hands as big as dinner plates, could unload dishes at 200 degrees like they were cool to the touch, and he played the harmonica and sang the blues and made like $2,000 a year, an old black man with kind yellow eyes. I'm not saying that everyone was perfect or always nice—we fought some Sundays like madmen. When the rush got to be too much you'd get in each other's way, and if you dropped an order or broke a glass in the dining room there was hell to pay. But mostly we did our jobs and got along fine, the way people are supposed to and almost never do.

But nothing lasts forever.

The week between Christmas and New Year's is slow in the pancake business. People take off from their jobs and eat at home. Richie was off so I got his hours, which was good because I almost had the five hundred dollars I needed for the Buick I had my eye on. So at 8 a.m. on the Tuesday after

Christmas I came into work and, first thing, Kay pulls me aside and says,

"Watch your step, Tony."

"What's up?"

Kay didn't say anything but nodded toward the kitchen.

In the fry corner, where Ray would usually be working—cooking or prepping, swaying to Fats Domino or Al Green—stood Misty, dressed in white, wearing a toque, and looking like a fool.

"What the hell is going on? What's she doing back there?"

"She's the new assistant manager. She's learning the grill."

"No way. Where's Ray?"

"Gone. He walked out. Fernandez put her back there with him and told Ray to teach her eggs. He picked up his radio and left."

"He quit? He didn't quit did he?"

"Who knows? Ray's proud. He's not going to work with her," Kay couldn't say Misty's name. "We might not see him again."

"That's bad. Assistant manager? What's going on with that?"

"Fernandez is sticking her in our faces. And in his wife's. They must be getting divorced. Anyway tread lightly. Everyone's on edge."

I did. We all walked around in shock. It was like coming home from school and finding a new Mom cooking dinner. Or like the time in second grade my beautiful teacher Miss Yaskowitz got married and became Mrs. Grant and then one Monday just wasn't there anymore. I cried for a week and fell behind in school and never caught up. I don't like change. You get comfortable with the way things are and then someone comes along and ruins it.

Misty stayed in the fry corner until the breakfast rush got going, then Bob took over. She made pancakes. They looked burned to me. Fernandez was back there too, showing off, running the Wheel and yelling at Ellis for plates. The dining room was a mess. Everyone was grumpy, and I felt like I had syrup in my bones—I couldn't move and broke two glasses. Ray didn't come back, not that day, and not for the rest of the month.

A few years after I'd left Perkins Pancake House, when I was done with the little bit of college I could stomach, I got drafted into the Army. They made me a rifleman, an eleven-bravo as they called it, taught me how to shoot an M-16, detonate a Claymore mine, fling a hand grenade far enough so as not to blow myself up, other useful things. It was a sure bet that I was headed to Vietnam, a prospect I viewed with indifference, just like everything else. Then my turn came around for KP. You had a week of it back then, getting up at 3 a.m. to peel potatoes and slice onions, grill bacon and make about five hundred scrambled eggs. Most guys hated KP, but I liked it. Being around food was natural for me; it was work I'd always done. Me and the staff sergeant in charge of the kitchen hit it off right away. He was stealing a couple hundred dollars' worth of meat every day and selling it in Leesville, also dealing dope to the NCO's out of his kitchen. I didn't care. He liked me because I worked hard and was good with a knife. After my week of KP was up, Sergeant Klein asked Top if he could keep me on in the kitchen, and that's what probably saved my life. I did my tour, twenty months total, with what they call the "clerks and jerks," the guys mostly out of the line of fire who serve the meals and process the 2173's for the dead—good duty. The point is that being good at something, even something lowly like cooking eggs, can save your life—can make your life. I didn't realize how true this was when I was sixteen, but living makes you smarter, or it should anyway.

We didn't see Ray again until the beginning of February. January had been a miserable month at PPH. First of all, it snowed every day, and my Skylark, running slick tires and a four-cylinder engine, gave me fits getting to work. I was back in school, so I worked nights, but I was always on the job Sundays for the tips. Misty was off the grill, downstairs, Kay said, working on the books. Who knew what she was working on, but she wasn't cooking eggs. Bob was in Ray's old place, and he was fine, and Mel, sometimes drunk, shared the pancake cooking with a new guy, I forget his name, who lasted about two weeks. That's how it goes. Short-order cooking attracts a lot of transients, but then so does long-order cooking. It's the heat maybe, or the rush, or the bad pay. A lot of jobs are that—you stick them out for a while and then move on.

Anyhow, that Sunday in February I looked out into the foyer and there's Ray, dressed as if for church, with a nice-looking woman and a couple of kids. I waved but he wasn't looking at me. He was smiling, like he always did, listening to his inner R&B, talking to his wife. The hostess was new too, so she didn't just bring him in ahead of the others, which would have been right, and so Ray waited, a black man with his family, standing among the white folks, everyone dressed up. He stood there and looked like he belonged, and I wondered what he felt, I wondered if he wished he were in the kitchen again, rolling through the orders. But Ray was just smiling. I could tell he didn't care about waiting for a table and that he wasn't wishing anything at all. He was just being Ray. And right then, standing by my bus cart, I knew my own days at Perkins Pancake House were numbered.

Who Do You Love?

I have a lot of bad habits, but the worst one is that I fall in love with other men's wives. This, I'm pretty sure, is a facet of my repressed homosexuality—I love the husbands but can't act on my love in a physical way so instead I project my feelings in a confused fashion onto the women *they* love. On the other hand, I don't like men at all. Not just physically. I don't even like men as friends. I have never had a male friend in my life. Like many men, I prefer the company of women. But every woman I have ever liked has also served as an object of tortured sexual fascination for me. I will say to them—*isn't it great how we are just friends?*—and they will think I mean it, but every minute that I'm with them and lying about how I feel, I'm really thinking about how much I would like to undress them and touch their bodies. I never feel this way about men. Men disgust me. This disgust, I am certain, arises from my discomfort with my own body. I feel an unconscious attraction to men but then project my own repulsive physical person onto them—the hairs that grow out of my ears for example, or those blotches on my chest that arise and recede as if with the phases of the moon. Then when I try to imagine sex with a man—which image I never can attain because of the strength of my disgust—what I end up with is the idea of having sex with my own body, an idea that is frankly sickening.

Women are a different story. I have always felt attracted to them, despite my repressed attraction for men. Age is no obstacle, aside from the very young or the very old. Nor is body type. I have had lurid fantasies about overweight women and about women who are within the ideal range of height and weight. Race and ethnicity aren't factors at all, though I have a hard time imagining sexual relations with women who wear religious clothing. However, as a matter of record, I have never had sex with a woman who did not resemble me in nearly every respect. I imagine this must be another form of projection. I search out a man who is like me, but then find myself driven by social norms and my own conscience to switch the gender of my love object. My wives have all been of average height and weight, perhaps ten pounds overweight, just as I am, with medium-length brown hair and hazel eyes.

So much about love and sex is confounding.

Many years ago I found myself, as usual, falling in love with another man's wife. His name was Thomas, although after studying theosophy and in particular after reading the works of Madame Blavatsky, he shorted his name to Om. His wife was a vivacious Italian girl named Anna. Om made a precarious living as a potter, crafting fertility symbols, yonis and lignums, out of thick red clay imported from Sedona. Anna worked at the local mall selling cosmetics; her coloring was perfect for modeling the products she sold— high cheekbones, henna-colored hair, eyes that were nearly black. I actually met her before I met Thomas. I was shopping for a bottle of cologne for a woman I was seeing at the time. We got to talking. Anna was stunning, but more touching than her beauty was her elegance. Cosmetic-counter women dress well, in heels and stockings. Anna had a great figure, slender arms and the kind of legs for which narrow impractical shoes are designed. As she walked around her little island of beauty products she seemed like a goddess, like Cybele, dispensing not only mascara but also forgetfulness and yearning. She had a big diamond on her left hand so I asked her what her husband did for a living. We then had one of those small-world kinds of moments. Her husband, Thomas, had given up a lucrative career in real estate law for 'his' art. It just so happened that I was back in school after a decade of travelling around the Northeast with a rock band. I wasn't a musician but a sound tech. Anyway, life on the road had gotten to be tedious, and I had enrolled at UMass to finish my degree in physics. Between customers, Anna would glide back to where I was perched on the make-up stool pretending to examine the myriad shades of eyeliners, and she would tell me something else about her remarkable husband. For my part, I was trying to memorize the shape of her lips and the perfect line of her legs so that I could think about them later. Eventually I bought three ounces of *Rapture* for sixty-two dollars, nearly a week's TA salary back then, but I also carried off Anna's and Thomas' phone number.

I waited a few days and then called. Anna picked up the phone and said that she had told Thomas all about me. He wanted to meet me and could I drive up for dinner that Saturday. Of course, I was delighted.

They lived in a rented house in Cummings, miles from the university, on five acres of run-down horse farm. Thomas was a tall, gangly guy with an unkempt beard and a pony tail. He came to the door wearing a red robe made from some flimsy fabric, rayon maybe, and he was as pale as a ghost—he looked like a choir-boy from a madhouse. But he was also handsome—not a word I used often, but apt. He had white, straight teeth, a long patrician nose, bright blue eyes—he looked like Harrison Ford might look if he lost twenty pounds and joined an ashram.

Anna was at the market.

Thomas told me about his new name and asked if I would mind calling him Om.

"I'm getting used to it."

"Sure 'Om' it is. Like the chant."

"No, not at all. I'm not a Buddhist. I'm a Jungian. But Jung says you're supposed to take a new name. I've been reborn. I took Om as my name on Anna's suggestion."

"Fine. Om it is. I'm Zebadiah but I go by Zeke."

"That's unusual."

"My parents were proto-hippies. My sister is named Daffodil. Or was. She went to court and had it changed to Connie."

"Gift of God."

"I beg your pardon."

"That's what your name means. Gift of God."

"Huh. Bet my folks didn't know that. They were atheists."

"We know things that we don't know we know."

Om, Thomas, preferred gnomic phrases. Simple declarative sentences. Paradoxes. He struck me as foolish, but compelling.

He had a big studio behind the house in what had been a barn. He had done the conversion work himself. He had woodworking tools, a welding kit, potter's wheels, kilns, piles of scrap wood and steel plates, iron sculptures and half-finished furniture. His sculpture was of high quality but of dubious aesthetic value—it looked mass produced and personalized at the same time. Like he had copied the designs from a book with an eye for detail but no sense of how the parts made up a coherent whole.

He walked around the studio pointing to his work, indicating how each piece fit into a comprehensive personal theology that he was working out with the help of Blavatsky, Khrishnamurti, Anne Conway, and Jacob Bohme.

He had notebooks filled with drawings and scribbled passages of obscure texts and boxes connected by jagged lines; they looked like force fields or Feynman diagrams. One page said "All is TWO" followed by a red-ink sketch of a three-dimensional Rosicrucian cross and a hovering Chagall figure of an angel. Another notebook had page after page of nude studies—they were of Anna—and I looked carefully through these when Om went to the bathroom.

When he came out we sat on the floor Zen-style. I mean, Om did. I stretched out and leaned against the couch. Thomas had fierce eyes that seemed to bore into my head. To say he was intense doesn't come close to the feeling he engendered. He asked me questions, at first general ones about my background, and then personal questions about my family, and, finally, invasive questions. What moved me? Was I religious? Did I enjoy sex? Had I ever had sex with a man? I was uncomfortable at first, and then angry. As I became more hesitant in my answers he grabbed my shoulders in both of his powerful hands and pulled me into an embrace that was unnerving. He said, "You shouldn't worry about how you feel; it's normal. Don't be ashamed, there's nothing to be afraid of." I said that I didn't know what he was talking about. He ignored me and went to start dinner.

Anna returned with groceries and wine. I felt I could see through her clothes. I imagined her breasts, her stomach—then I was ashamed and looked away. She wore jeans and a loose flannel shirt; her hair was tied up with a piece of ribbon, a swirl of reddish waves with single strands accentuating her thin neck. Nothing in the world is more beautiful than a woman's neck. Thomas changed from his prayer robe into cut offs and a tee shirt. He was heavily muscled, lean and strong looking. The two of them made a handsome couple, but I noticed that they didn't touch—in the kitchen, as I sat sipping wine, they eased past one another like sleek race cars avoiding a crash. They spoke to each other like siblings rather than lovers. There was baby talk, which I found touching, but sad. Anna made pasta and Thomas made a salad. We ate on a paint-splattered table, talking and listening to Freddie Hubbard. After dinner I cleared the table while Thomas fired up a bong with a chip of hash. Anna didn't smoke. I took one hit to be polite but I didn't inhale. When he was high Thomas started to meditate and softly chant; he put a cassette of bird calls on the stereo that I found annoying. Birds outside are one thing, but half an hour of chirping in a smoky kitchen gave me a headache. We moved to the living room. I sat on the couch next to Anna. After a while she tucked her feet under my legs. We weren't talking. I could smell her. From my hours in cosmetics I could tell she was wearing Chanel. Later that night, after Thomas fell asleep, Anna kissed me, not passionately, but like a close friend. A few weeks later, after several identical nights—pasta, wine, hash, bird calls and Om's passage into a trance state—Anna and I went outside and had sex against a tree.

After that early spring night, Anna and I started to meet several times a week. We would go for coffee or take a walk. Sometimes we checked into a motel. I'd never had sex like the sex I had with Anna. We didn't have anything in common but Thomas, and we talked about him as if he were the reason we were together. Anna loved him. I said that I loved him too. This wasn't true, but my need was so great, my emptiness so deep, that I couldn't bring myself to disagree with anything Anna said. The truth was that I thought Thomas was insane, though in an interesting way. Om was a genius, Anna told me. He had visions, she said. He was saintly, a martyr to art and to love. He let her do as she wished. He didn't constrain her. For example, she told me, he knew about us and approved.

"You told him?"

"Oh no. He just knows."

"We've been discreet. How could he know?"

"He sees into my soul. Probably into yours too."

"What does that mean? Is he a mind reader?"

"I told you, Thomas is a spiritual being. He reads people. Their auras. Their hearts."

"And he doesn't care that I eat his food and screw his wife?"

"Not at all. He loves you. I told him you were a good man, gentle, but lonely. He understands that. He wants me to help you."

"Help me what? I'm fine. I'm in love with you, Anna."

"I know that. But I love him. And he loves you. And you love him too I think. We all feel something for one another. That's why he can share me with you."

"That sounds odd to me. I mean, I *like* your husband, but I don't love him. It's you I want."

"It doesn't work that way with us. And we're not married."

"You're not?" This seemed like good news.

"We have a bond that's spiritual. But we don't feel the need to have a civil wedding."

"You seem married to me. The ring and all."

"It's just a sign. Listen, I want you to tell me what you think of Thomas. How does he make you feel?"

"I don't know. He's interesting, talented. Dynamic. Good looking I guess. Why?"

"He wants you to know him. I can tell he feels something for you, something special. That's why I went with you."

"What are you talking about?"

"Seeing you together, I knew you were kindred souls. Music moves you, and art. And you were attracted to me, just like Thomas. I could see he was in love with you, right from the beginning. I wanted to be the bond between the two of you."

"Anna, hold on. You've lost me. He *loves* me? What are you saying? He's gay? Because I'm not. It's you I'm interested in, not him."

"'Gay'? What a word. We aren't made like that, those categories don't mean anything. We're spirits. Our bodies are extraneous. We drift about in emptiness until we find a companion soul. We love the spirit of a person, not the body. Do you really think you can possess me by penetrating my body? That's like thinking you make art by putting paint on a canvas. Love and beauty aren't physical."

"You could have fooled me. I mean, you did fool me. I thought you were turned on by me."

"Pleasure is important to me. But it isn't everything. You can make love to me all you want. But I want you to know that Thomas needs you too. You can't have me alone. He and I are on a journey together. We're the same being."

"He needs me for what?"

"I don't know. You have to ask him."

"I can't do that."

"Are you afraid?"

"It's worse than that."

"Than being afraid? Of what you might feel? Of who you might be inside?"

"That's right. Like every other sane person I'm afraid of who I might be, or of what I might become. And unless you're really an angel, and you might be one for all I know, you're afraid as well. That's the way we're made."

"There's no shame in loving someone."

"So you say. But there is. We've made it a shame. We're supposed to pair off two by two, remember, and march into the ark and keep the world full of lonely people like ourselves."

"That's not for Thomas or for me. Or for you. Come on. Let's go home."

"Home? Your home isn't my home."

"But it could be. Whatever you want is possible, Zeke."

"How about if you come home with me? That's what I want."

"No you don't. Not really."

When we got back to Cummings, to the farm, Thomas wasn't around. Anna led me upstairs to their bedroom. She undressed me and then took off her clothes. We lay down on the bed. It was messy. I could tell the sheets hadn't been changed in a long time. It felt strange to lay my head on Thomas's pillow, to hold his wife in my arms, to smell him, that acrid odor of him, just as I pulled Anna on top of me. Her musk, the scent of her hair, the coffee on her breath, all of them were drowned out by the rankness of his smell. I felt ill, and then Anna eased me into her body, rocking me gently, whispering my name. As I started to come I ground my teeth and said her name, and then, horribly, his—*Om*, my god, *Om*. Anna laughed and pushed against me hard and raked her nails across my chest. And I did it again. The words came out of me in a voice that wasn't mine. It was *her* I felt. But the words were wrenched out of my guts like I had been torn open. My chest was bleeding; there was blood on Anna's stomach and on the bed. She was tearing at my chest and face and I was crying in pain and something else—*Om* I kept saying, meaning *Oh my god*. But I couldn't control my voice—I came again and again until the room grew dark and Anna's laughter and my own crying and someone else's laughter broke across my body like a great wave and I let go and fell and poured into her, or into him, poured myself out into emptiness.

Axioms

The moon shone like water on the white comforter.

I couldn't sleep. We had finished a bottle of wine at dinner—a cheap Shiraz from Chile, not my favorite. There had been an hour set aside for reading. She flipped through the *Times* while I waded into another in a series of Scandinavian detective novels—brooding books written by men whose names I couldn't recall when someone at work would ask me if I had read anything good lately. This one was by a Norwegian and had won the prestigious Nils Gunderwald Prize. On the first page the alcoholic detective is called to a small village near the town of Fredrikstad, south of Oslo. There he encounters both a decapitated body and an old school acquaintance. The body hasn't decomposed in the winter cold. The detective, who, we are informed, smokes Gitanes and drinks too much Dovgan vodka, recognizes the dead woman as an ex-mistress, a physician with whom he had a brief affair between the second and third of his failed marriages. Her name was Kristen. The school chum—the translator has used the word "chum" as well as "corpulent" and "tendentious" to describe the detective's friend—has also been in love with Kristen and may be the father of her son, now a young man studying archeology at the University of Gothenburg.

My wife asks me if I know the capital of Burkina Faso. I tell her Ouagadougou. I spell it. She says that can't be right. And I say that I may have misspelled the name, but that I am quite certain Ouagadougou is correct. She looks at me through her reading glasses—she is very beautiful and, as is always the case, looking at her reminds me of my failures. She pushes her hair back and then does that thing women do which requires them to raise their arms above their heads and simultaneously bare their abdomens and accentuate their breasts while casually tying their hair into a kind of half-knot that invites pulling, a triple-erotic whammy. Without smiling my wife points to my book and asks me if I like it. But she gets up and walks into the kitchen before I can formulate an answer that will seem both thoughtful and approving without at the same time suggesting that she should read the book since I know she has despised Scandinavian writers since learning of Knut Hamsun's Nazi sympathies.

I pretend to read but strain to hear what my wife is saying. She is speaking softly on her cell phone, standing near the back door, right next to the Super Quiet Maytag dishwasher her parents gave us for our first anniversary. The morose detective has been attacked in his hotel room, or perhaps he has merely fallen down drunk. It is snowing and all of the usual outdoor sounds are muted. The hotel is seedy, which seems out of character given what I know of Norway. Water is rushing up through the sink, gurgling in a ghostly way. My wife is laughing and I think how she never laughs with me. I call out to her, just her first initial, *R*, and ask if she would bring me a beer. She doesn't respond. The dishwasher is coming to the point in its cycle that I refer to as its death throes—the glassware is clinking too loudly, and I think of how upset my wife will be if anything breaks. The *chum*, whose name is Eriksson, discovers the unconscious detective and slaps his face to "bring him about." The translator, I begin to feel, lacks sensitivity for English idioms.

I wonder about this. There is a picture of the translator at the back of the book, but no picture of the author. This too seems odd. When my wife comes back into the room, without my beer but with a glass of water for herself, I smile and mention to her the infelicities of the translation. I'm hoping to say something witty enough to make her laugh, just as I heard her laugh a moment ago. She says that "bring him about" is fine, she's used the phrase herself. I ask her about the circumstances and she shrugs. I mention that consciousness involves the interconnected firings of billions of neurons as well as the leaching of chemicals, like serotonin, across neural membranes. She says that she is going to bed. I get a beer.

My wife takes her time in the bathroom. Our apartment is downtown and small. I work uptown but enjoy taking the subway. My wife is a stay-at-home wife, that's what I call her, perhaps with a trace of irony. She feels that she has worked hard all of her life and deserves to take a sabbatical. I have three weeks off each year. During that time we drive to Ohio to visit my wife's extended family. Every year we rent a couple of cabins on Lake Williams. While my wife goes shopping with her mother, I teach my nephews how to play chess. They find the game boring and dislike my enthusiasm. When my wife leaves the bathroom she is wrapped in a towel. The floor is wet and her clothes are strewn about like flowers.

R lies across the bed nude. I have brushed my teeth thoroughly and used the last half ounce of Listerine. I begin to kiss her, but she rolls away and pushes down under the sheets. I do the same. I say that I love her. She looks at me and rubs her hand across my face. It is a mistake to do so but I repeat the words. My wife is a quiet person, undemonstrative. Her manner of keeping still and being inward was once attractive to me. She turns toward the wall and seems to say that she loves me, but the rustle of the bedclothes makes it hard to hear what she is saying. I say 'good' and turn my back to her, hoping that I will sleep. I don't.

In the morning I will take my novel back to the library, unfinished. If she has time, my wife will empty the dishwasher. We need wine so I will stop at the shop on the corner for a bottle. Perhaps white, a Sauvignon Blanc. The *Times* arrives early, but I will have left for work by the time the blue cylinder is tossed onto our stoop.

What our hearts most desire eludes us. Joy flies from us like the airy light of a full moon in March.

Scene of the Crime

The suburbs aren't for everybody. For one thing there's the problem of getting to work. Then there's the lack of amenities like restaurants, museums, bars, libraries, or playgrounds. Of course some of these things can be found, but they suffer from the blandness of all things sub- or ex-urban. The library in Marlton, for example, only stocks best sellers. The playgrounds are new, but focused on child safety rather than on enjoyment. The roads are crammed from morning until night, and the only decent place to eat is Rusty's Steakhouse. We're vegetarians.

On the other hand, the houses are big, the yards have grass, and the rents are a third of what we were paying in Philadelphia. So we moved.

The kids were happy to have their own room and a swing set. My wife enjoyed the sounds of birds in the morning. I had a long bus ride to work, but plenty of time to read best sellers. We planted a lilac that first summer, forsythia, wisteria and a few grape vines. The soil was black and rich, unlike the sparse sandy dirt of our tiny city yard. Things grew. There were lots of bugs, but the exterminator came twice a month.

"I love it here," my wife said.

"We love the yard," said my kids.

"The neighbors seem hostile," I said.

The couple next door had filled their yard with the relics of American blue-collar life—there were two pop-up trailers, an above-ground swimming pool, a trampoline, rabbit hutches (they ate the bunnies, a fact that gave my daughters nightmares), a motorcycle, two junk cars, a woodpile, a metal shed whose roof had rusted through, a collapsed log playhouse, and three dogs whose barking soon negated our ability to listen to song sparrows and finches. Sid and Nancy were in their forties and not visibly employed. Sid was overweight and appeared in his backyard early each morning wearing a jogging suit of what appeared to be white silk. He tinkered with his engines in that way people have of starting them, revving them, shutting them off and then repeating the process. Nancy never left the house. But then no one left the house in our suburban neighborhood. Dogs were let out unattended; no one walked or jogged. Cars slid out of the driveway and eight hours later slid back in. Doors went up automatically, then they closed. Windshields were heavily tinted. Shades were drawn year round. Pumpkins, flags, and white lights made their appearance at the appropriate times, but we never saw anyone actually put them out. Everyone was hunkered down, waiting out the weather, or the administration, the recession, or whatever war was being fought. I walked up the street—there were no sidewalks—to Route 70 to catch the bus. If I saw Sid I'd wave and shout 'Have a great day' but he never acknowledged my greeting. I noticed that his head was shaved and that it glowed in the morning light.

Yes, there were advantages. But living in the suburbs felt strange. I never had lived outside of the city before. We kept waking up in the middle of the night listening to the wind. I don't recall ever having heard the wind during my years of living in city apartments. When my wife and children were gone,

I would wander through the house vaguely opening and shutting closet doors. We had a linen closet that I was using to store canned food. No one complained about my poor renditions of "Body and Soul" on the saxophone or the loud radio broadcasts of Phillies games. We could do as we pleased. And yet my wife and I admitted that we felt tense. I was worried about the children playing in the front yard. People drove too fast, as if on some vital errand. When my girls set up a lemonade stand in front of the house no one stopped, and on Halloween, despite our orange lights and carefully-carved pumpkins, no children came to the door—we ate the Three Musketeers ourselves. That night, always among my favorite of the year for its intimation of deep autumn, was empty and silent and strangely haunted.

"I still like it," my wife said.

"We do too, sort of," said the girls.

"There's something not quite right about this," I thought.

On Thanksgiving, Sid emptied his swimming pool, pumping thirty-five hundred gallons of chlorine-laced water directly into our back yard. When I saw the black hose snaking from his pool under the fence that divided our properties I was flabbergasted. Who would do such a thing? I trotted next door and rang the bell. No one answered. I went around back. Sid was in his shed, staining an Adirondack chair. The dogs came running, snarling at my legs.

"What's up?" Sid said.

"Are you kidding me? You're draining your pool into my yard. It'll kill the grass. The plants."

"Whattaya mean? I don't know what you're talking about."

"Look," I grabbed his meaty arm.

"Keep your fucking hands off me. And get outta my yard."

"All right. But I'm calling the cops."

"Call 'em. What the fuck. I drain my pool wherever I want."

"We'll see about that."

"Scram, you punk."

"Punk? You're calling me a punk? I'm forty years old. I have two kids. I've got a job, which is more than I can say for some people."

"What's that supposed to mean?"

"It means I don't lounge around in a track suit all day. It means I work. You know, for a living."

Sid took a swipe at me, a big roundhouse that missed by a mile. I'm no fighter so I beat it, mutts nipping at my heels.

I jogged home and dialed the non-emergency number. A woman answered. She asked me if it was an emergency.

"Yes and no."

"Excuse me?"

"It's important, but no one is dying."

"What happened? Car stolen? Break in? Mugging?"

"My neighbor is emptying his swimming pool into my backyard."

"Say again?"

"His pool. Thousands of gallons of water. As we speak they're sluicing into my rosebushes. It's a flood. I need an officer to come out here and restrain him."

"Sorry, but we don't have the manpower for that sort of thing. Just talk to your neighbor. Be reasonable about it."

"Reasonable? It's Sid that's being unreasonable. He tried to hit me."

"Sid?"

"My neighbor. The guy who's killing my grass."

"He hit you?"

"No, he missed. But he would have."

"It isn't assault if you weren't hurt."

"That's a weird distinction. If he'd shot me I couldn't of called you."

"What's your name sir?"

I ignored this. My wife didn't like me to give my name out over the phone.

"So you aren't going to help me?"

"I'll mention your problem to my boss. But it's Thanksgiving. I wouldn't count on a patrol car. We're a small force covering a lot of area. We've got break-ins, rapes, assaults where someone does get hurt, you name it."

"I thought Marlton was safe. The sign says 'A Safe Place to Raise a Family.'"

"What sign is that?"

"The one on Route 65. Right past Cherry Hill. Big, with trees and laughing children on a see-saw. Rapes? There's actually raping going on?"

"Not often. But still. You can't use manpower for lawn floods. I'll check the statutes later, but I don't think what your neighbor is doing is a crime."

I hung up.

I bit my hand in frustration. Yelled at my kids to keep quiet. The water was splashing against our sliding glass door. It was dark brown and carried broken bits of our honeysuckle.

I ran to the garage and found my ax. We were going to cut our own Christmas tree that year. In keeping with the rustic nature of our new suburban life.

I slogged through what was left of my backyard. Sid was pumping the accelerator on one of his ATV's. I pulled the black drain pipe from his pool under our red cedar fence, pulled it like I would the head of some poisonous snake, and whacked at it with the ax. My wife opened the sliding door to yell at me. I ignored her. I hacked into the soft rubber, punching deep divots into the wet grass and covering myself in mud. When I cut though it a torrent of water sprayed into my face. I pushed the now-smaller hose back under the fence. The water was pouring into Sid's yard. I felt triumphant.

I went inside. My clothes were a ruin. I took a shower in scalding water. Opened a beer. A police car pulled into my driveway.

The cops, two cops, ambled past our picture window. They looked exactly the way I knew suburban cops would look. They were gigantic, "larger than life," was the phrase that popped into my head as I went to the door. They wore those thick leather belts that contain fifty different apparatuses for maiming another human being—guns, knives, Mace, blackjacks, ten-pound flashlights, clubs, and two pairs of handcuffs to slap on the corpse.

"Mr. Clayton?"

"That's me."

"Could you step outside please?"

"Why don't you come in? Can I get you a beer?"

They looked at one another.

"Step outside Mr. Clayton, and leave the bottle here." One of the behemoths gently but firmly took my Miller High Life bottle and set it on the table. I stepped outside.

"Do you have some identification?"

"Me? Of course, I mean, like what? Driver's license?"

"Yes sir. A driver's license. Most people don't carry their birth certificates around with them."

I chuckled at this. "No, I suppose not. But I just showered. It's inside, in my wallet."

"Okay. We'll worry about that later. My partner needs to look in your garage. Does he have permission to do so?"

"Why does he have to look in there? It's just a garage. Tools, golf clubs, maybe a car."

"Mr. Clayton, are you going to cooperate with this investigation or are you not?"

"Investigation? What investigation? Maybe you should tell me what this is about. I thought you were here because I called the police earlier."

"You called? When was that?"

"I think an hour ago. My neighbor is, was, in the process of destroying my backyard, so I called the non-emergency number."

"No record of that. Can my partner go into your garage or not? We will get a subpoena if we need one, but it would be easier if you cooperated."

"Subpoena? What did I do? I mean, you should be talking to Sid there. See him? He's the fat guy in the track suit. There, over the fence."

Sid was peering at us, smiling at me.

The cops didn't look.

"Okay," the cop whose name tag read Delbert said to the other. "Let's go."

They started toward their car, a long sleek black Taurus bristling with antennas and with a shotgun clipped to the steel cage separating the front seat from the back.

"All right, all right. Go inside. Look to your heart's content. But you won't find anything in there."

"Have a look-see Mel," said Delbert.

Mel went in and came out ten seconds later with my ax.

"Here it is Del." Mel was wearing plastic gloves, the kind doctors wear when they pinch your prostate.

"That's my ax."

"It's your ax? So you admit this is your ax?"

"Why shouldn't I? It's mine. It came out of my garage. What's the big deal?"

"The big deal Mr. Clayton is assault with a deadly weapon." Mel pulled out a piece of paper and read me my rights. Delbert put handcuffs on me. My girls were looking out the window, crying. My wife was standing behind them, shaking her head.

"This is a joke, right? I cut my neighbor's hose so his filthy water wouldn't ruin my yard. Who did I assault?"

"*Whom*," said Delbert.

"Jesus H. Christ." I know cops don't approve of blasphemy, but I hate being corrected.

"Watch your mouth, Mr. Clayton."

"*Whom* did I assault, allegedly?"

"That's for the court to decide, Mr. Clayton. We have a complaint, we have a witness, and we have the weapon. So, no, this isn't a joke."

"Does that man look like he's been hit with an ax?" I pointed toward Sid. He was leering at me, miming handcuffed wrists.

The cops finally looked over. Sid waved. The cops smiled and waved back.

"Hey Sid, how's it hanging?" shouted Delbert.

"You know. No complaints. You got the guy?" Sid was giddy; he was rolling his big bloodshot eyes at us like a madman.

"Well, presumption of innocence and all, but, yeah, we got the ax."

"That's a relief. It's unsettling for Nancy you know, living next to these people."

That's when I lost it.

"What are you talking about? You bum! *Nancy*, who the hell is *Nancy*? I've never seen any fucking Nancy. Does she even know that we live here? A goddamn shut-in is what she is, and you're a bum! The two of you are *bums*!" For some reason I felt compelled to repeat the word "bum." It sounded right, and it conveyed what I had long felt about Sid and everyone else in this godforsaken place—they were bums.

Mel pulled hard on my arm and told me to shut up. My wife was banging on the widow. I could hear my children wailing.

"You asshole. My wife's an *invalid*." Sid pronounced the word as 'in*val*id,' with the accent on the second syllable, which must have been a slip of the tongue. He bolted from his perch on the fence and trotted toward us. Three of us, soon to be four, and three more, in the shadows of the house: a tableau, etched against the fake blue siding of our rancher, which was, I decided, ugly and cheap looking—the vinyl windows, the treeless vista, the dying grass. In the city the sky always looks the same—dull white, shading toward gray. Here you could actually look up and see that Marlton Glen and all of southern New Jersey was covered with greasy light, as if the land was wrapped in a filthy rag. I was taking this in, ignoring the tug of the handcuffs, the banging and crying. I was in a fugue state—was that the word?—delirious, hallucinatory. My mind had torqued out, I had slipped out of gear and was whirling like an untethered flywheel, spinning but going nowhere. I noted without interest that people were coming out of their houses, gathering in the street. There was a crowd in front of my house—a dozen people, not one of whom I had ever seen before. Sid was still shouting, walking toward us. His voice bent in the air. Dopplered.

"An in*val*id! An invalid!" He was chanting, wagging his head, spuming like a great fish, shucking his silken jacket.

I squared my shoulders.

"Hold on Sid. We got this under control. Stay back." Delbert let go of my arm and put his hand on his nightstick. I knew the cop would hit me first.

Mel whined, "Clayton, that was a rotten thing to say. My wife is housebound.

You better apologize!"

Too late for that. "You people are nuts. I've seen her walking around. Once anyway. And so what? My wife's got asthma. My daughter's allergic to peanuts. And you're dumping your pool in my yard." I almost wept just thinking about that water. My grass. I moved here to grow grass and now it was dead. Water was oozing around the side of the house, headed downhill toward the road and the small knot of neighbors, all of whom I now noticed were dressed in bathrobes and slippers, strange indoor creatures clustered right in the middle of Marlton Glen Way. A guy in front yelled to Sid and gave him thumbs up.

The front door opened. My wife fell out onto the porch. Sid kept yelling. His face was red and his shaved head shone with perspiration. Time stopped. Mel held out a hand to my wife and pulled her to her feet. Delbert tugged me toward the patrol car; the engine was still running, the radio pulsing waves of static into the dead air. Sid stopped his blather and began to pant like one of his Rottweilers. Delbert let go of me and put a meaty hand on Sid's chest. He said something, but my ears were ringing—my heart was in overdrive. My wife appeared to be hugging Mel. The group in the middle of the street scurried toward us as a UPS truck came flying down the street.

My wife broke away from Mel and collapsed. The UPS truck stopped in front of our house. The driver threw open the back door of the van and pulled out a big box. He trotted up to our front door, paying no attention to the cops or the crowd, or Sid, or me in handcuffs. He spoke to my wife, asking her to sign for the package. She shook her head no, so Mel signed. The driver opened the front door to put the box inside and the kids ran out, hysterical, and fell on their mother. The UPS guy smiled and ran back to his truck, threw it into gear and sped off, scattering the growing contingent of gawking neighbors.

"Bulbs" I said to Delbert.

"What?"

"Those are bulbs for my yard. Tulips. Ten kinds. We thought it would look nice to have them in the front yard."

"My wife and I got irises. Can't get enough of them." He said this as he was pushing me into the patrol car.

The kids stopped crying and watched me duck into the back seat, behind the mesh cage and the shotgun. One of the people in the street applauded, at least it sounded that way.

Then Sid said, "Wait a minute. Del, hold on."

"What? Hold what?"

"I'm not pressing charges. I changed my mind. Let him go." Sid was looking at my kids holding onto their mother.

"You can't change your mind. If he assaulted you we're taking him in."

"He didn't. I mean, not exactly."

Delbert sighed and said "What are you saying Sid? Did you call or not?"

"Yeah, yeah I called. He was chopping up my discharge hose. But he didn't physically attack me."

"Well Jesus H. Christ. That's a hell of a thing Sid. Me and Mel come running over here, holiday and all, arrest this guy, and you're saying all he did was chop your hose? What the hell." Delbert looked at Mel who shrugged and picked my wife up again. The kids got quiet.

"Okay." Delbert pulled me out of the car, none too gently. He took the handcuffs off of me and threw them on the front seat of the cruiser. Mel walked over to Sid and started to say something, but thought better of it. He climbed into the passenger side of the car and mumbled into the radio. After a minute Delbert got in and backed the car out of the driveway. On the street he made a gesture at the crowd and they started to break up, but not before one of them shot me the bird.

I rubbed my wrists, just the way they do on TV, and walked over to my wife. She didn't look at me. The kids backed away.

Sid walked a few steps toward us. He held out his hand and offered it to me. I didn't move. He put his hand in his pocket and nodded his head, turned around and walked back around the cedar fence and into his yard. A minute later I heard his motorcycle revving. On, off, on, off. By now the torrent of pool water had slowed to a trickle. Most of my top soil and all of my compost had washed into the street. I suppose our roses were washed away as well. I no longer cared. I put the ax in the garage and went into the house.

My wife and kids were sitting on the couch reading a book. Everyone appeared calm.

I looked at them, and they just kept reading. It was starting to rain, a sound I've always loved.

"We could get a puppy," I said.

The girls smiled. My wife smiled. I got a beer and turned on the TV.

There was nothing on.

January

"Um. That's nice. Don't stop."
"You like that?"
"Um."
"You're lovely."
"I know."
"Sexy."
"Shut up."
"Sorry."

"It's cold in here."
"Come to bed."
"In a minute."
"What are you doing?"
"Getting coffee. Want some?"
"Tea."
"Tea?"
"I'm Irish."
"Still."

"Then forget it."

"Just kidding."

"Milk and sugar."

"Coming right up."

"It's so fucking cold."

"It'll warm up."

"You teach school, right?"

"I told you that last night."

"I'm a little unclear on last night."

"Really?"

"I didn't mean it like that."

"You? What do you do? I don't think it came up."

"I'm a musician. I told you."

"You're kidding. Oh shit."

"What?"

"I slept with a musician."

"Not much sleeping."

"You seemed nice at the party."

"I'm not that kind of musician."

"There's only one kind."

"I play the viola."

"No."

"In the Janos Quartet."

"No way."

"Someday I will."

"What's your name again?"

"Gregory."

"Liz, in case you forgot."

"Sun feels nice," said Liz.

"Dim though. January's awful."

"That's such a guy thing to say. I love January. Snow especially."

"I hate snow. It's dirty."

"Not at first. At first it's clean."

"This city's shit."

"No it's not. It's not."

"Where're you from?"

"Originally?"

"Depends on what you mean. Not where you were born. Where you grew up."

"Same dif. Boston."

"That's a great city."

"Not really."

"Boston's world-class."

"Meaning what?"

"Orchestra for one. I love orchestras, obviously. And museums. Harvard."

"Harvard? Give me a break."

"What's your family do?"

"They work. Play. Copulate. Fight. The usual."

"Seriously."

"Seriously. Dad's a professor. Mom too."

"Harvard?"

"What's up with you and Harvard? No, they both teach at a real school. BU."

"Oh, I get it."

"What do you get?"

"You're jealous."

"Of Harvard? Gregory, you must be kidding."

"You want to go out?" asked Gregory.

"No thank you."

"You gonna stay in bed all day?"

"I might. I have to teach tomorrow."

"I can't stay."

"Fine."

"You like kids?"

"You like music?"

"They're different."

"No shit."

"No, I mean, music is easy. Kids."

"Are easy too. I love them."

"Good thing."

"Don't mind me, I'm grouchy sometimes."

"That's okay. You were nice last night."

"Was I?"

"You remember what you said?"

"When?"

"When we first met. At the party."

"Vaguely. You looked handsome."

"That's what you said."

"What else?"

"You said I was the most interesting man there."

"I must have been drunk. That's a bit much."

"I was though. The most interesting man. It was a horrible party."

"I don't like parties."

"Why'd you go? If you hate them?"

"Not hate. Dislike. I went because I'm lonely."

"How could you be lonely?"

"Everyone is lonely."

"You're a beautiful woman."

"I'm not, but if I were, what difference would that make?"

"You could meet people. Men."

"I don't want to meet people. Or men."

"Then what's this?"

"It was fun."

"That's all?"

"What, do you want to get married?"

"I see your point."

"Mostly alone is best for me. But not always."

"Sure. But not for me."

"What do you mean?"

"I don't like to be alone."

"But you are."

" . . . ."

"You're not?"

"I'm married. Technically."

"What does that mean?"

"I'm kind of separated."

"Kind of separated? That's weird."

"Not that weird. It happens."

"I mean it's a surprise. You don't seem married."

"How does married seem to you?"

"I don't know. Sad. Inhibited. Loyal."

"We're going through a hard patch."

"And I'm easing your way?"

"That's a trick question."

"In these situations that's the only kind."

"You're upset? I'm surprised."

"I'm not upset. A little disappointed is all."

"Did you want to get married? To a musician?"

"Maybe. I mean, who knows? We were good together."

"The heart most desires what eludes it; it despises what it may possess."

"Who said that?"

"I don't know. I think I made it up."

"It's a mean thing to say."

"Sorry."

"I know, I was being casual. But I have to protect myself. My heart."

"I understand. Sorry."

"Please don't say that."

"Sorry."

"Married? For how long?"

"Fifteen years."

"Jesus. To the same person?"

"Of course."

"So I was the object of your adultery."

"That's hardly fair. You picked me up."

"I did not. You invited me to leave the party."

"Not right away."

"What's that got to do with it? You could have told me."

"What?"

"That you were married."

"But I wanted you."

"*Wanted*? Jesus. I haven't heard that in a while."

"It's true."

"Wanted how? To take to bed?"

"No. Not entirely. To be with. To talk to."

"Please. You hardly spoke a word all night."

"So what? You didn't either."

"I told you everything about my life."

"It wasn't much."

"There's not much to tell. I'm twenty-six."

"I'm too old for you."

"How old are you?"

"Forty."

"You look younger."

"Thank you."

"It wasn't a compliment. I meant immature."

"Ouch. You're angry."

"No. A little. Yes."

"May I be honest?"

"It would be refreshing."

"I'll ignore that. What's wrong with what I did?"

"Nothing really. I was surprised is all. Maybe I was hoping for more."

"What about you? Do you have someone?"

"No. There's a guy I see, not often."

"And?"

"Nothing. He's strange, but sweet. It's nothing."

"You never know. My wife and I met in an odd way. We weren't right for each other. Then we were for a long time. And now."

"How did you meet?"

"On an airplane."

"Like, what, sitting together?"

"She was a stewardess. Hostess. Whatever they call them."

"And you were the navigator."

"A passenger. We hit it off over Kansas City."

"It's so sad."

"Thanks, I mean, that's nice of you."

"No. Not you and your wife. Everything."

"Everything is sad is hardly profound."

"I mean, love is sad. Relationships. You're one example."

"Well, what do you expect? Love is complicated."

"Why? People say that, but not why. What's so complicated?"

"Because it requires commitment. And that's nearly impossible."

"Who says? I think that's really bullshit."

"Look Elizabeth, think what you will. You've never been married."

"Don't call me that."

"What?"

"Elizabeth. It's too queenly. I'm plain Liz."

"You told me that was your name."

"That was before."

"Okay, sorry."

"And don't say 'sorry.' I hate that word. I hate people telling me they're sorry."

"Sorry. No, I mean…"

"How do you know?"

"What?"

"That I've never been married."

"Have you?"

"Of course not. If I had been, I still would be."

"You can't just assert that, like some law of nature."

"Believe me Greg, what I assert I mean. I don't fuck around."

"Okay. But you'll see. My wife and I meant always to be married. To be in love."

"I'll bet stewardesses get a lot of dates."

"What makes you say so?"

"They're like nurses. Authority figures. Men love authority figures. Women cops have to beat men off."

"Jesus."

"So what went wrong?"

"Drift. A lot of life is just drifting. You wake up a different person."

"That's the most pathetic thing I've ever heard."

"You're in a nasty mood."

"No. You're dishonest, and whiney. What's 'drift' have to do with love?"

"You care for somebody and they change. Or you do. It happens."

"Not to me."

"It just did."

"What do you mean?"

"Am I still the most interesting man in the room?"

"Afraid so."

"That was nice. Thank you."

"You're welcome."

"So."

"You want me to go now."

"Soon. I have to vacuum."

"Is our fight over?"

"I suppose. Do you want it to be?"

"Can I see you again?"

"Maybe. I don't know. Tell me something."

"Anything at all."

"What do you want? Not from me in particular, but what moves you?"

"Is this a test? So I can come back?"

"No. I'd like to know you better. What do you care about?"

"That's a tough one. Music. I think music is most important to me now. It consumes me."

"For what? I mean, it consumes you in terms of a job, or for its beauty, why does it?"

"Both. A job, for sure, also for itself. I love the repertoire that I play. I love to practice and to listen to others. I enjoy the instrument. Playing gives me peace."

"That's good. Forgive me though Greg, but is that it? What about other people, a family? What about your wife, or ex-wife? Do you have children, or do you want to?"

"No children. We had plans, you know, but we were both busy. You have to have money and time. We didn't. But, sure, sometime."

"But you're forty. How much time is there?"

"Plenty. People have children later in life now. There's no rush."

"And your wife?"

"Probably not going to work out. I just don't feel it, you know?"

"You don't seem upset."

"I am, I'm very upset."

"You should be. I mean, all those years, just a waste."

"They weren't wasted. You can't say things like that. Suppose you gave up teaching and went to law school. Would your earlier life be wasted?"

"Of course it would. You can't just change everything around. Life's short."

"Well, I don't see things the way you do. Change is part of it. You have to adapt."

"Greg, look, I'm not a lizard, changing my colors to fit in. I don't have to adapt. What I have to do is stay on course. Do good for others, for my kids. Fall in love if I can, marry. Have kids. Die. That's what I have to do. Adapting is for lower-order organisms."

"You're a little weird, you know that? In a nice sort of way. I've never met anybody so young who was so conservative."

"I'm not conservative. I'm reactionary."

"You vote for Reagan?"

"Christ, no. I mean I believe in tradition. I'm traditional."

"You voted for Dukakis?"

"Never mind who I voted for. What do you care?"

"Joking. Well, I'm traditional too. But traditions change. Culture gets transformed. You can't deny it. Do you listen to madrigals on the radio? Do you read George Eliot? Brush your teeth with your finger? Change is good."

"Whatever. I disbelieve in it. That's what my Dad says, disbelieve. He's funny. You and he would hate each other. Anyway, he'd hate you."

"That's a hell of a thing to say."

"It's true. He's never liked any man I've brought home. And he certainly wouldn't be thrilled to see me with a musician."

"Violist."

"Doesn't matter. He likes people who are solid, make their living in honest ways. With their hands."

95

"You think I play with my feet?"

"You know what I mean, an honest job."

"What, like plumbers? He wants you to marry a plumber?"

"As a matter of fact, a plumber would be fine. Or a farmer. A teacher. Someone who works."

"I work."

"You play. You're a sort of artist. A craftsman. Unless you compose music."

"I don't. Man, you can be a real hardass."

"Bitch. You mean I can be a bitch. You can say it. I won't pout."

"I know what you're doing."

"What?"

"Distancing yourself. You're making me out to be a low-life so you won't feel so bad when I leave. You won't think maybe you missed out on something."

"That's exactly right."

"You're being nasty now."

"No, not at all. I mean it. That is what I'm doing. You're married so I can't count on you. Never have I slept with a married man. Well, once before. That was different though. So I'm pushing you away. You're really perceptive."

"Different how?"

"What?"

"How was the other married man you slept with different than me?"

"The man was different, but that's not what you mean is it? You mean the circumstances."

"The circumstances, yes."

"He loved me. That was the difference."

"Maybe he just said that to get you into bed."

"We never went to bed, never had sex. I slept with him, but he didn't touch me."

"Huh. How does that work?"

"We had a relationship. He loved me, but he told me he couldn't leave his wife. He loved her too. It was heartbreaking. More for him than for me."

"Why's that? I mean you were caught in the middle."

"Not one bit. There was no middle. It was a triangle. The forces were equal in all directions."

"Don't tell me you loved his wife?"

"I did. And she reciprocated. And no, that wasn't physical either. We all three were in love, that's all. We cared deeply for each other. But he was married to her and not to me. That was bad luck, but not a tragedy. I knew how it would turn out."

"How did it turn out?"

"Guess."

"He left you. You never saw him again?"

"I never saw either one of them again. He came to my house, here, it was three years ago. Also in January. Martin Luther King Day. Also snowy. There was so much snow on the Avenue you couldn't hear the cars. He knocked on the door. It was late afternoon. I wasn't expecting him. I could see that he had been crying. His eyes were red. He was pale. My heart broke for him. I knew why he was here. I knew he had to stop coming or we would do something irrevocable. He loved his wife. So he just came in and we lay down together on the bed. He held me. I could feel his tears on my neck. A long time. Hours maybe, or it seemed that way. He had his coat on, it seemed odd, it was warm in the room, but he couldn't do anything normal, so he had on his coat, his shoes, but still I could feel his body under all the clothes. I wanted him and I didn't if that makes any sense. The temptation to touch him was powerful, but I knew that would make things more difficult, so I just lay there, still, hardly breathing, wishing after a while that he would get it over with so I could be alone and maybe cry, maybe not. You can't believe the things I felt, how confused I was, relieved and sad, aching for him and wanting him to go away, angry and also touched and pleased that someone could love me so much. No one ever loved me as much. Finally, after forever, it seemed all day, the sun was burning through the window, the ice was dripping from the eaves, you could hear the ice breaking and falling down the front of the house onto the sidewalk, sharp cracks, and the creaking of the roof under the snow, and the kids outside, screaming because there was no school, running across the park, flinging snowballs and building snowmen and making snow forts. This was what was running through my mind, images of what was outside, because in here time had stopped, like this was a spaceship headed to Saturn and we were frozen asleep but somehow still conscious, bound to make this two-hundred year voyage to the rings of Saturn, and we could still remember, at least I could, what it sounded like back on earth when kids played in the snow. And what was he thinking? I couldn't imagine. The same things probably. We always thought the same things. If we were together and I wanted to have dinner, I knew he would too. So he wanted to let go of me and dry his eyes and go home to his wife and kids. And he would be able to sit at the kitchen table with a glass of wine and explain to his wife how he felt as he visited me for the last time, and she would nod in the thoughtful way she had—I loved how she listened, how full and deep her attention was, how she seemed to care about everything I felt, like it was a matter of life and death. And I'd have the same glass of wine, sit at the table, stare into the dark panels of the front window, out at the freezing black January night and just try to stay alive.

Sure enough, when we couldn't take it any longer, I couldn't, he disengaged himself and got up. He didn't say one word to me. What could he say? I didn't want to hear anything. Most of all I kept thinking to myself that if he said he were sorry, if he uttered that word, then I would hate him for the rest of my life. But he knew. He was smart about me, and he didn't say he was sorry. He took my hand and I got up off the bed. I nearly fell over. I was weak and dizzy. The kids were yelling, and I smiled at him, and when he smiled back we both knew that it was the yelling of the children that had cheered us up, nothing else. And he led me to the kitchen, poured me a glass of water and got one for himself. We tapped glasses like we always had before, and we said *kampai* or something else like we always did, it was one of our little jokes, and we drank the water down as if it would heal us, as if it would make everything all right, as if it weren't shitty Philadelphia tap water but champagne. And then he leaned into me and kissed me on the mouth and pulled away and said *goodbye my love*. His last three words to me. And he turned away from me without looking back and walked out the door and down the steps. I walked to the window and looked down and could just see him as he went out the front door, pulling on his blue watch cap, one I had given him for his birthday since he owned no warm clothes and would walk around freezing, and he was pulling on the cap and walking toward his car— I could see it down the block, badly parked. He was a terrible driver. I worried he would have an accident on the icy roads, but it was no longer my concern what twists his life would take, where he would go or who he would speak to or who else he might love. I was out of it. And I rapped hard on the window, so hard the glass rattled, but of course in the thick air and snow he couldn't hear me and he didn't turn, didn't turn, walked, didn't turn, then, right as he reached the car, as he was pulling on the door, he looked up at the window, probably seeing only empty glass and not me, he looked up and waved once, stiffly, as if he were boarding the spacecraft again, alone this time, alone, completely alone."

"Jesus, I'm sorry."

"What?"

"I said I'm sorry."

"God I hate that."

"What?"

"People saying they're sorry."

"It's a tragic story. I mean, it's totally tragic what happened to you, the loss."

"Oh my dear Greg. Now I'm sorry."

"Why? What are you talking about?"

"You've missed it, you've missed the point. There's nothing tragic about that story. Tragedy is fate. I knew what I was doing, we all did. It's just my story. Everyone has one like it, or will. If you live long enough you can't avoid it."

"But you loved him?"

"Yes. I loved him very much."

"And he loved you."

"Yes."

"Then I'm dense."

"No Greg, you're not dense, just not deep."

"Bitch."

Mr. Stinky

Elvin couldn't back the twenty-four footer up so he drove around the block until he found a pull through spot. The F350 was bigger than anything Elvin had ever driven, and with the Zinger attached there was no way he could park in the tiny spaces behind the municipal building. Doris got out and watched her husband pull in so as to minimize the chances of snagging another car or the curb. The rig was new—six thousand highway miles—and it had cost them one hundred percent of Elvin's buy-out, so they weren't taking any chances. It was insured, but with a $500 deductible. Anyway, Elvin was a careful man.

Harlan looked like a nice town. That's what Doris said to Elvin when they pulled off the state road and onto Main Street.

"Looks nice, El. Look at the Victorian houses there, those old maples and elms. In the autumn light everything is glowing."

"Hmm. Kind of small. We better check in with the police if we're going to park in town."

Elvin was still self-conscious about the rig and how proprietary it looked when you parked it downtown in Iowa or Nebraska, in out-of-the way places where strangers stood out. Doris didn't think you had to check into every new town, like you were some kind of alien, but Elvin insisted that it was the polite thing to do.

"They don't know us, Dor, and with the New Mexico plates they might think we're here to make trouble. A lot of people in this part of the country don't even know that New Mexico is part of America."

Doris thought this was a silly notion, but she wasn't given to arguing with her husband about little things.

"Okay, El. You go to the police station, and I'll walk down there to the library, get the lay of the place. Come down and we'll get things set up for tomorrow."

Doris walked away. Elvin watched her go. She was humoring him, and he was grateful. He'd always been the nervous type, and a homebody. Living on the road, being retired, always being an outsider—these things were difficult for Elvin. Doris, he thought, had always been more outgoing and quite a bit braver. But he thought he wanted this new life as much as Doris; he needed it in fact, and the little discomforts weren't so bad.

Elvin locked up the Zinger, set the alarm, and ambled over to the police station.

Six months before, Elvin had been given an ultimatum at his job. He'd been teaching math and science at the Curtis Middle School in Albuquerque for thirty-five years, and he wasn't eager to retire. He enjoyed his work, liked the students, but above all needed the settled routine of a job. Nothing gave him more pleasure than rising with the sun every morning, eating his cornflakes and reading the newspaper, then heading off to do something that felt useful. He enjoyed the company of his colleagues, the free lunches and the suburban quiet of the campus. Elvin wasn't cut out for a high-pressure job, nor did he much care about status. He liked being what he was—a quietly competent teacher of algebra and earth science to well-behaved boys and girls whose parents valued education.

In January, just after the Martin Luther King weekend, the Head of School had called him and asked that Elvin make an appointment through the school secretary to "spend a little time" with him in his office. Dr. Boland, as he insisted on being called, was new to Curtis. He wasn't even fifty years old, and, Elvin knew, he was the type of educator who had spent little time in the classroom. When he had been hired by the Board of Trustees to replace Bill Thomason, a career history teacher who had reluctantly agreed to manage Curtis on an interim basis, Ned Boland had made a point of distancing himself from "traditional" and "outmoded" assumptions about the mission of private schools in a "global economy." The phrase "global economy" had come up dozens of times during Boland's two days of interviews at the school. The younger instructors found him energetic, bright, and "a visionary." Older teachers, like Elvin, were less enthusiastic. In particular, Elvin had been outspoken during faculty meetings about the need for Curtis to take a cautious approach toward adopting technology-centered forms of instruction. At one especially contentious meeting called by the department chairs to collect feedback on Dr. Boland's candidacy, Elvin had violated his usual policy of making only occasional, quiet comments, and suggested that hiring Boland would set the Curtis School on a new course, one that might compromise the original mission of the school, a mission that stressed the development of the students' character, critical thinking ability, and independent judgment. Later, after the meeting adjourned, Elvin was haunted by his ill-chosen words: "I don't think that Dr. Boland's educational philosophy can be reconciled with the vision of this school's founders. Doctor Reynolds and his cofounders wanted to create a learning environment focused on opportunities to develop a young person's character, not their future earning potential." There had been an embarrassed silence when Elvin had uttered these intemperate words. He still believed they were true, but some things are better left unsaid.

Face to face, Elvin had to admit that Boland was an impressive person. His longish dark brown hair was swept back from a high, and, Elvin noted, unwrinkled forehead; he had blue eyes, flushed cheeks, and perfect white teeth. He was wearing a monogrammed gray Oxford shirt with a tie pin—it was a very nice shirt—creased gray twill trousers and tasseled black loafers. Elvin was wearing what he thought of as his teaching uniform: wrinkled khakis from Target, a no-iron white shirt, and his only tie, a thin, black, rayon cheapie from K-Mart. He always wore sneakers to teach, but he'd put on a pair of scuffed desert boots that had been stashed in his file cabinet for twenty years. They were, Elvin knew, men of different worlds. But no one intimidated Elvin anymore; he'd been around for too long, seen too many administrators come and go, usually to better jobs in bigger cities, and, in any case, Elvin knew that he was good at what he did—he'd been New Mexico Teacher of the Year just three years before, had won a Presidential Citation for his work teaching geology to seventh graders, and he was adored by most of his kids. What could Boland do to him?

"Elvin, glad you could drop by," Dr. Boland made this remark as he swiveled around in his chair, turning his back on one of the three computer screens he kept on an enormous maple credenza which, rumor had it, cost the school ten thousand dollars.

"Nice of you to invite me." Elvin hoped he had kept the irony out of his voice. He was busy and hoped this meeting would end quickly.

"You know why I asked you in today?" Boland got up and moved to one of two leather wing chairs that fronted his capacious desk.

"Not sure. Probably to get acquainted with the faculty. Hear my views on the state of the school. Something along those lines."

Boland chuckled. "Not quite. Actually I wanted to have you come in so I could tell you about an exciting opportunity that's being offered to a select few of the more experienced faculty. The Board has given me the okay on this initiative, just did in fact, and you are among the first teachers I wanted to talk with. Get your views on it, that sort of thing."

"Sounds exciting. I'm all ears." Elvin felt queasy as he said this. More computers, larger classes, increased enrollment—it had to be something like this. The Board was strictly bottom line, local real estate developers and members of the "business community"—men and women who'd attended Curtis, gone to decent colleges and come back to town to get rich. Their rise in fortunes had coincided with Albuquerque's rapid, if unsustainable, growth— it was the booming aught's, speculation had replaced reason, and Elvin, who was no business whiz but did understand basic economics, figured that the bubble would burst at some point and that lots of ordinary people would get hurt. Curtis was well-endowed, but everyone who loved the place worried that its money was tied up in risky investments.

"Great to hear. So. You know that I was brought on both to oversee the educational end of things and to look after the institution's financial health. They're related of course. I realize that some of you classroom teachers prefer not to think about the nuts and bolts of running a place like this . . ."

"What makes you say so? I mean, what makes you think I care any less about the school's financial health than anyone else?" Elvin couldn't keep a bit of pique out of his voice. He was sensitive to condescension, and that was what he heard.

"No offense. I just mean that your focus is on the students—as it should be—but I have to worry about the long-term health of the institution."

"Of Curtis. You mean of Curtis."

"Of course I do."

"You keep saying 'the institution.' We're a school. It seems important to keep that in mind."

"A school. Yes, of course this is a school. But it's more than that. It has responsibilities. To the Board, to alumni, to the community."

"But above all, to the students. Those enrolled here, now. And to their parents. I'm not trying to be argumentative, but I think it's important in any such discussion about what's good and what's bad to put the students first."

"And you think I don't?" Boland was reddening. Elvin was sorry he'd become contentious. He had meant to listen.

"Not at all. I apologize. You were saying? About the opportunity?"

Dr. Boland got up and walked over to his small refrigerator, took out a Diet Coke and raised his eyebrow at Elvin.

"No thanks," Elvin felt nervous now, unsure of himself.

Boland went to his desk and came back with a file. He sat down in front of Elvin, crossed his legs, and opened the file. He took out a piece of paper and handed it to Elvin.

"Let me say first off how much you mean to this inst…to Curtis. You're clearly a superior classroom teacher. A credit to our mission. I want that out front, just so you know."

"Thanks, I mean, I love the school, the kids. It's great to work here. The colleagues." Elvin trailed off. Boland wasn't listening.

"So, Elvin, you are what, sixty-four?"

"Actually, sixty-five. Just turned. Doesn't feel like it, but yes, I'm getting older."

"Have you given any thought to retirement?"

"No. None."

"Well, it's a good time to do so. We've put together a nice package. For you and the others over 62. Half a year's salary. Benefits for two years,

106

including medical, so you can get set up, find your own carrier. In your case the offer is . . ." Boland looked at the file he was holding, took a piece of paper from his desk and scribbled a number on it, handed the paper to Elvin.

Elvin couldn't focus. It was just a number. It meant nothing to him.

"What do you think?" Boland was smiling; his crossed leg was bouncing up and down. Elvin was staring at the man's socks. They were pink. He'd never seen pink socks on a grown man. He couldn't think about anything else but the socks.

"You're wearing pink socks," said Elvin.

Boland's leg stopped bouncing. "Excuse me?"

"I said, I notice you're wearing pink socks. I don't know why I noticed that, but it sort of popped out at me. Mine are white. See?" He couldn't imagine why he did so, but Elvin pulled up his trouser leg to show Dr. Boland his white cotton socks. It was, he thought later, the stupidest thing he'd ever done in his life.

"I don't see what this has to do with anything." Boland was flustered. "I've just made a proposal. A generous proposal. I'm asking you what you think of it."

Elvin got up. He stashed the piece of paper in his pocket. "Sorry. I'm at a loss. Please, forgive me. This is a surprise. A shock. May I think about it, talk to my wife?" Elvin was already at the door.

"Of course. Take your time. And Elvin? This isn't a judgment on your abilities. No one doubts your excellence as an instructor. It's just that the budget, well, you understand. There's twelve of you, experienced . . ." Boland didn't finish. Elvin walked out the door, down the long corridor, and into the bright sunlight.

The F350 with the Zinger had cost $80,000, more or less. Cash. Doris hated their house and was glad to sell it. They'd lived in it for fifteen years and were able to sell it for a substantial profit. Within one month Elvin and Doris went from being homeowners, employees, and citizens of Albuquerque to being nomads. Elvin used the word 'vagabond' but Doris didn't like it.

"We're nomads." Yes, that sounded right to Doris, nomads, like Lord Byron in Greece, or Thoreau wandering around Cape Cod.

"Or Genghis Khan marauding across Asia" said Elvin.

"Whatever. Come on Elvin, don't be so staid. This is a wonderful opportunity for us. Mr. Stinky goes on the road. And I'm your sidekick, Mrs. Stinky."

"That won't do. You have to have a different name. Ms. Chatterbox?"

"Not bad. But will the children know what a chatterbox is? How about Mrs. Butterfly"?

"Too, I don't know, too mushy. You don't look like a butterfly."

They batted around more names and ended up with Mrs. Mouse. Doris would wear whiskers and her old Disney ears. Neither one of them liked the name much but Doris tried to make the best of it.

"Kids love mice," said Doris.

"That's a myth. No one likes mice. They carry disease and drop little fecal raisins all over the kitchen. It's Disney propaganda that mice are loveable."

"Rabbits are raisins. Mice leave caraway seeds. 'Droppings' my mother used to say. As if mice had slippery fingers. I don't like mice myself. They're vermin."

"So, not Mrs. Mouse?"

"No, Elvin." Doris hugged her husband and nuzzled his neck. "Sweetheart, I'll always be Mrs. Stinky."

Doris had been a librarian when she married Elvin. She'd worked in the downtown branch of the public library, in the children's section. Elvin had never been married, wasn't particularly social, and wasn't, he knew, especially good looking. Doris had been married for a while when she was younger, to a college teacher, but it hadn't worked out.

"I liked you right away," Doris told Elvin later on, after they'd had a couple of cups of coffee at the Route 66 Diner. "I could tell you had a sense of humor, and I loved your music."

"That's what women say about homely men. That they're funny."

"No, Elvin, that's what men say about homely women."

"Well, that's not you. You're pretty. Beautiful." Elvin had been embarrassed to say this, but it was true. Doris was a fine-looking woman, tall and well-formed. And she'd read everything.

"You're so knowledgeable. I mean, I'm one-dimensional. Science, that's it. And I'm not even good at math so my science is flabby."

"Flabby science. I like that. You know about the hedgehog and the fox right?"

"No I don't."

"The fox knows many things, but the hedgehog knows one thing. Being a dilettante isn't that great. I wouldn't mind being an expert at something. The history of art maybe, or of dance. But I'm all over the place. You seem mature to me. And that's a good thing."

Mature. Elvin at nearly fifty had liked the sound of that.

Elvin was—smitten? Was that the word for it? Doris was younger than he was, but she seemed genuinely to admire him—to find him interesting. This was incomprehensible. They courted in the old fashioned way, movies and dinners, long walks along the Rio Grande. Doris told stories, and did it with the whole bag of tricks—voices and accents and dramatic intonations. And

Elvin played guitar—pretty well in fact. He'd played since he was a kid. He did a credible job with Doc Watson and Lightin' Hopkins and especially Leadbelly. But mostly he did kid's songs, funny ditties that he wrote or picked up from records. That was how Mr. Stinky was born. He'd started singing to his students as a break from the academic routine. Then he tried to sing for low-key events—a student's birthday party, and then a few times at the library. That was how he'd met Doris. Mr. Stinky had been doing a series of afternoon concerts at the downtown branch, and Doris was working children's books. They talked a little after the songs, hit it off in the low-key way that shy people have, and, after a few chats, Elvin worked up the nerve to ask Doris out for coffee. Many coffees followed. And after the coffees, the first halting conversations, they began to feel comfortable with one another. Both had been lonely, that much was clear. As soon as they saw that they got along, that they didn't threaten one another's carefully constructed private worlds too much, they started to spend their Saturdays in Doris's Knob Hill *casita* entertaining one another—songs and stories, in the way that people once did who didn't have cable and movie theatres. They clicked. They both hated television—Elvin hadn't owned one for years—and pop culture, and crowds, and shopping, and loud people. Both of them had given up going to restaurants and bars long before. They like to stay at home, and so they did. They made up their own culture, their own world. The sort of thing that is hermetic but totally satisfying.

Elvin stepped up to the front desk in the Harlan Police Station. He took off his hat and cleared his throat. Policemen made him nervous.

"Can I help you?" The officer on the desk was a large woman, a sergeant judging by her stripes. Her name was Roselle.

"Yes, good morning. My name is Elvin Williams. My wife and I just arrived in town. We have an RV. It's parked out front there?" Elvin's voice rose steadily as he spoke.

"Yes? Is there a problem?"

"Oh no. It's just that my wife and I will be performing. At the library. And we'd like to park overnight. Out front. There's no RV Park in town. We hoped." Elvin couldn't find the right words. This often happened to him now, in his new life. There had been some slippage, some loosening of the way he operated in the world. Perhaps this was to be expected.

"Well, Mr. Williams, you're welcome to park overnight. We appreciate the heads up. At the library you say? Are you, what, a writer?"

"Oh no. Not at all. My wife and I tell stories. To children. I mean, she tells stories, and I sing songs. For young children. It's really very . . ." What was the word for what they did? Simple? Foolish? It was easier before when he taught science. "We're troubadours." That seemed right.

Sergeant Roselle raised her eyebrows and looked, for the first time, right at Elvin. "Troubadours? That sounds . . ." She didn't finish, but Elvin got the idea—"unusual" or "odd" was what she meant to say.

"Yes, it is. All of those things." Elvin smiled, so did the policeman, and then Elvin said thank you, and walked out the door.

It had taken a month for Elvin to decide what to do about Boland's retirement offer. "Severance package" was what Doris called it, making it sound as if her husband were an executive in an important company and was being given generous amounts of money and valuable stock options to clear the way for new blood.

"I'm old, they want me gone. It's not that complicated."

"Come on El, don't look at it like that. This is an opportunity. Half-a-year's pay! Why that's a lot of money. We can travel. You've always wanted to see the country."

It's true that Elvin had told Doris when they married that he wanted more than anything to drive around the United States, to visit Civil War battlefields, presidential libraries, art museums, and minor league baseball parks. But that was a long time ago. His ambition had—what?—dried up? Or been replaced by a longing to continue living exactly the life he had been living since he'd wooed and won Doris. To keep going to work and coming home to their tidy bungalow and sitting in the den at night playing the guitar and reading poems aloud—all of the reassuring things that made Elvin's life, in his mind, perfect. He no longer wished to leave town, to go even to Santa Fe. How could he have ever imagined that visiting strange cities would be amusing? What was there to see really? People, it appeared, were the same everywhere—angry, disillusioned, and self-absorbed. No, he'd changed his mind about his plans, but Elvin was ashamed to admit this fact to Doris. He didn't wish to unsettle his wife, or to detract from the pleasure she might take in imagining a life of adventure with him.

"Boland as much as told me I was finished. I could hang on for a while, but I'd only embarrass myself. I love the school too much to be a burden."

"That's not true. That's just not true El. Nobody thinks that."

"Boland does. And the Board. And it's not just me, the whole bunch of us old timers. We've become obsolete."

"Boland! Who's he to judge you? He just arrived at Curtis. Why he's still wet behind the ears—who cares what he thinks?"

"Doris, you're missing the point, he runs things now. He's the boss, and aside from the Board and the Treasurer, he reports to no one. Look at what this document says. Paragraph fourteen. 'This is a one-time offer. No promise of future employment beyond this contract year can be guaranteed to any member of the faculty or staff of Curtis Academy, as is stipulated on page 27 of the Faculty-Staff Handbook.'"

"That's boilerplate. We have that same understanding at the Library. I mean, who can't be fired at a moment's notice?"

"It never was this way, Hon. I had security because I did a good job. But that's not enough any longer. Things are different in education now. Public and private, all of us are under scrutiny. Somehow people have decided that we're not pulling our societal weight. Ever since the testing got out of control, or the charter schools took over. I don't know when or why, but it's different. I'm old, and I cost a lot in benefits, and I don't know much about computers, and I don't even have my master's degree." Elvin was depressing himself.

"Don't turn yourself into a cause Elvin. And don't beat yourself up because you spent your time teaching instead of getting meaningless credentials. Let's just take the money, Elvin. Let's get out of here! I'm fifty years old. I want to do things with the rest of my life. Let's go on the road. We can improvise."

"Jesus, Doris. I'm not Jack Kerouac. I'm a teacher. I don't want to wing it for the rest of my life; I want to live just like I'm living now."

"Well, darling, I've got news for you. You can't. They've pushed you out the door. So shut it, and let's find out what's on the other side."

On the other side of the door was heartache: bills, insurance premiums, lines at the Social Security office, phone calls to TIAA-CREF, arguments with Doris, tearful goodbyes with students and colleagues, cold memos from Personnel, phony 'celebrations' of a lifetime of hard work and dedication— all of it wearisome and sad and poignant to an extent that Elvin never would have guessed such a change could be. He had no idea how attached he was to the identity he'd crafted over four decades; shucking it off was more like removing his skin than removing his clothes. He bled for a while, wept quietly during sleepless nights, then, the day after graduation, he finished packing up his office, throwing away nearly everything but his books, and drove home from work for the last time.

"Elvin, hey, here we are." Doris was in the Harlan Community Library leaning on the front desk and talking to a thin, gray-haired woman. Both of them smiled at Elvin as he walked into the cool dim light of the old brownstone building. Elvin loved old public buildings like this one—they reflected an optimism that was now mostly lost. Solidity married to style seemed almost quaint in an age that valued neither.

"Elvin, this is Joanne Sealy, she's the librarian in these parts. Joanne this is Elvin, *aka* Mr. Stinky."

Joanne had a warm, small-town smile. The kind of smile that says 'you're not one of us yet, but you could be.' Elvin had grown up in suburban New Jersey and remembered the way it felt to stand in the front yard with his parents as they exchanged gossip with neighbors. His parents had a way of making such exchanges seem worthwhile, as if you really could 'take the time' to listen to someone you hardly knew, as if time could be stopped, the evening arrested in its anxious flight to somewhere else.

"Glad to meet you. I prefer Elvin actually. The other is my stage name. Though I've never been on stage. I guess Doris told you about our little act."

"Yes, and I have to say it sounds delightful. We're a small community. Harlan mostly services the farms here in the county, but there are a fair number of young children living in town. I'm sure they're looking forward to hearing your songs and stories."

"It was nice of you to agree to have us. We love Iowa. The country is so pretty."

"If you like corn. But we do have some charming back roads, and if you continue west you'll enjoy the drive along the Missouri. That's where I'm

114

from originally, Council Bluffs. Much prettier there, but this is fine as well."

Doris put her arm through Elvin's and said, "We're just driving for now, no special destination. Elvin was a teacher for many years, and we enjoy children. The songs and stories just give us a reason to stop. West sounds nice, but we may go north. Elvin would love to see Lake Superior. Wouldn't you, Elvin?"

Elvin admitted that he wouldn't mind, but he was also feeling uncomfortable. It seemed self-indulgent in an age of four-dollar-a-gallon gasoline to be 'just driving.' Shouldn't they have a destination? No grandkids to visit, no kids for that matter. No friends scattered around the country. Just the country itself, oversized and enigmatic. What must it have seemed like a hundred years ago to cross this black-soiled alluvial plain heading toward Oregon? You could still see wagon tracks outside of Harlan, deep ruts running across the small patches of public land that still existed in this sea of corn and soybeans, surplus crops subsidized by the taxpayer, a gesture toward the outmoded Jeffersonian idea of Americans as farmers. Elvin had forgotten in his long self-imposed exile how densely peopled the country was, how each two-lane blacktop in Oklahoma and Nebraska and Iowa bisected a thousand interchangeable towns, each with its bars and churches and Rexall and memorials to the boys killed in some war or other. He knew the geology intimately—he'd taught it for years— but of the millions of souls camped out on basin and range, on hillside and riverfront, people like Joanne what's-her-name here, smiling folks with jobs and lives and stories of their own, of this he had no inkling. Where did he fit in this great unraveling mosaic of a place? Standing there in Harlan, Iowa, half-listening to Doris narrating the tale of their travels, Elvin imagined he could feel the earth shifting under his feet, the tectonic plates of the Mississippi and Missouri Rivers banging against each other, perhaps edging toward some catastrophic collapse into the emptied out Cambrian-Ordovician aquifer, the one at this moment being sucked dry by these billions of soybean plants, by

115

these eager boosters who, Elvin noted, were breaking ground for a Wal-Mart on the outskirts of town, hoping for growth probably, or a better place to purchase discounted Chinese clothing. What did Elvin think he would find when he climbed into his obscenely large, gas-guzzling Ford and pulled his Zinger around the black tar roads of the upper Great Plains? Had he been looking for a way to fill the void that his life had become, or was he, as he had told Doris, eager to see what was going on in the American landscape, the one beyond the eastern shore of the Rio Grande? He no longer knew.

Later on, in their Zinger, taking up two parking spaces on East Street in Harlan, with everyone else in town at home, sitting around the dinner table discussing the price of crops, or the weather—Elvin imagined the kinds of conversations that people were having as vastly different from the kind he and Doris usually had, but who knew for sure what other Americans chatted about over their fried chicken and green bean salad—Doris served Elvin a nice casserole, his favorite, ham and potatoes and peas, and asked him, please, to tell her what was wrong.

"Sweetie, something is bothering you. You hardly said a word in the library today, and you've been moody all afternoon. This isn't like you El. You're the most engaging of men. I'm a little bit worried about you."

Elvin, as always, felt touched by his wife's solicitude, even as he was, he had to admit, annoyed by the presumption that his inner life should be a matter of public record. He was out of sorts, there was no doubt about it, but he didn't feel like talking about why because he didn't understand the causes, or perhaps because there was no cause at all.

Instead of answering the implied question, Elvin did a little deflecting. "Hey honey, you remember our first real date? Not the coffees downtown, but the first time we dressed up and went out?"

Doris laughed. "Indeed I do. Inauguration night. You took me to the

Rancher's Club. You had the rib eye. You were wearing your blue suit and those alligator boots, the ones I never could get used to."

"And you had the filet. You wore the yellow dress, soft and swirly. We danced to Phil Lank, remember? He had that Serbian drummer, and the big blond from Paris? She sang 'Route 66' about five times."

"That's because there were a bunch of Texans in the crowd that night. That lean fellow with the Adam's apple asked me to dance."

"And I said, 'Sorry partner, this gal's mine.'" They laughed at the memory.

"What made you think of that, El?"

"Just nothing really. It was fun was all. I knew we were going to be happy. And things were hopeful back then, like we hadn't turned this bad corner. That's a part of it too. Your own hope has to be part of a larger one. Maybe that's what's bothering me."

Doris smiled at her husband. She got up from the little dining table that pulled out of the trailer's side—the dining room was part of the living room which was also the bed room—and went back to the closet. She pulled out Elvin's Martin and handed it to him.

"Go ahead. Play some. I know it cheers you up."

Elvin loved the guitar. It had been his father's. Grayson Williams had been the first African-American to play with Tommy Tucker's Big Band in the 30's and 40's. Elvin's father had grown up playing jazz and blues and then swing; he'd taught music at Monmouth College after his retirement. Elvin hadn't had his father's gift, but he loved music, and found solace in playing, however badly he did it.

Elvin strummed a few chords. The instrument had a rich, sonorous tone— it was teak and maple, a dark sunburst dreadnought that Grayson Williams had purchased before World War II. It was worth as much as the Zinger. Elvin started to play "Puff the Magic Dragon," a song Doris enjoyed.

"Not Mr. Stinky. Play something serious. How about 'The Very Thought of You?'"

"I don't think I can Doris. I'm rusty. My fingers are like ropes."

"Go ahead. Play it for me." Elvin laughed at the line.

"What the hell. Here goes." Elvin started to play. Ray Noble had been an acquaintance of Elvin's father. Nat Cole had once sung the tune with Tommy Tucker's band, and though Elvin had been too young to have heard it, he'd owned the record as a kid and played it over and over. The song had run through his head for half his life. He couldn't do more than hint at the melody on the Martin, but it felt good to make the chords, to feel the sound grow out of the old, lovely instrument.

"That was nice, Elvin. You need to play more. And the music you like."

"Nice of you to say Doris, but it's too late for that. I'm going to stick to what I've always done best. I've been an entertainer all my life—not a scientist, not a scholar, not a musician—but a damn good entertainer."

"It really hurt you didn't it? I had no idea."

"What do you mean?"

"Boland. The way they made you retire. I thought you were okay with it. But you weren't. I'm sorry that I didn't know."

"Doris, please. I'm fine. It takes time to adjust." Elvin started to play an old song that he loved, a blues tune, one his father had taught him when Elvin was just learning to play. It was 'Corrine, Corrina,' and Elvin sang it with feeling. He had a nice baritone, a church voice, soulful and quietly powerful.

Doris teared up. Her husband was a proud man. She thought she could hear the pain in his voice.

"That was lovely."

Elvin was pleased, not only with the song, but with the repose he now felt, as if rehearsing some unknown person's misery had lifted a burden for him.

"Do you know that line from Leadbelly, 'Sometimes I take a great notion to drown'? You can hear it in his songs. That's what art is Doris, putting your heart into something, your pain. Singing is like that, blues or jazz, it doesn't matter. Teaching is like that too, if you do it well. That's what Boland doesn't get. To him and his ilk Curtis is a business. Education is just production, and I was an old, slow line worker. I love you Doris. You've got the best heart of anyone. To care about an old man like me. I'm not sad at all about this life. Or, I was, but it passed. I like Mr. Stinky, he brings laughter to children. We'll sing and tell our stories tomorrow just like we've been doing. But you know what I want to do?"

"What?"

"After a while longer, I want to go home again. Back to Albuquerque. Sell this thing and buy a little house. And then I want to see if anyone will have me, as a teacher. I want to teach again, Doris. I miss it too much. But only if you want to go back as well."

"I'd like that. The road gets old after a while."

"It does get old. And really, it's all the same isn't it? I mean, we're the same no matter where we are."

"That right El, we're the same. You and I are always going to be the same."

Elvin smiled at his wife and shut his eyes and played a soft blues he'd learned from his father—the first song he'd ever played well enough to feel in his bones. It was Doc Watson's "Worried No More."

As he sang Elvin knew that nothing else mattered.

Applebee's

Brad was in a bad mood after work. He usually was in a bad mood, especially on Fridays. I'd had a birthday the week before and some of the girls at the salon had chipped in for a gift card. I love gift cards—you can pick out what you want, but not just anything. Having some limits on what you can buy is good, at least for someone like me, a person who enjoys going out but has trouble making up her mind where. Anyway, I had $50 for Applebee's, which is pretty much my favorite place to go, so I asked Brad if he felt like eating out. He didn't. He doesn't enjoy going out at all, but he can be a good sport sometimes, and so he said, sure, let's go eat.

"I hate this place. Why do we always come here?" Brad started the minute we walked in the door. That's his way. The place was crowded; there were people sitting outside, smoking, talking, but this was to be expected since it was Friday night. We got in the door right away. The hostess told us ten minutes, which means twenty. That was fine with me. I like waiting for a table. You can chat a little and build up the anticipation.

"It's inexpensive. The food is good. What's wrong with it? I mean, we don't live in Denver. You live here this is pretty much it. McDonald's, Wendy's. But I like Applebee's."

Brad makes me feel defensive. But I was relaxed and ready to have a good time so I didn't let him get to me.

"Look around. What do you see?" Brad is a large man, with a loud voice. He doesn't tone it down in public places.

"People. Regular people like us. What are you talking about?"

"These aren't people. Look at them, chomping on their ribs. It's disgusting. The women are fatter than the men. I hate this place."

"I like it. It's families. There's three generations over there, gramps and granny, the kids, the grandkids. They're having fun. What's wrong with you?"

"It's ordinary. Here comes Babs."

The hostess came over. She was maybe seventeen. She was wearing a nice outfit, a little blue skirt and a clean blouse. She smiled and asked us how many were in our party. Brad held up two fingers, and I said "Just us two." The girl picked up two of the large plastic menus and led us into the back, away from the bar, which is exactly where I prefer to sit.

I smiled at the girl and said "Thanks." Brad left for the bathroom. He always goes right into the bathroom every time we go out. He says to wash his hands, but I think he doesn't like sitting with me for too long. That's what I think.

He came back just as the waitress arrived at the table.

"Hi. I'm Debbie. I'll be your server. What can I get you folks to drink?"

"I'll have a Bud Lite," I said.

"Water for me." Brad only drinks at home. He says that beer costs too much out, and he's right, but who wants to sit at Applebee's and drink ice water?

"I'll be right back with the drinks."

"Christ."

"What?"

"Did you see her shirt? It's filthy."

"So what? She's a waitress. You want her to wear a tutu?" I was still feeling pretty good.

"Maybe a clean shirt? Is that too much to ask?"

"It probably was clean three hours ago. Did you ever wait tables?"

"No, Meghan, I never waited tables. I suppose you did?"

"No, but I can imagine what it's like."

"You can imagine? Well imagine somebody waiting on you who wears clean clothes. Can you imagine that?"

I ignored this remark. Brad can be difficult. But I knew he had a long week, and you have to humor your husband when he's like this.

"Here she comes."

"Here we are, folks. One Bud Lite and one water."

"Thank you."

"Ah, I don't care for lemon in my water."

"I'm sorry. Can I get you another?"

"No. It's all right."

"May I take your order?"

"Could we have a minute more? This menu's longer than the Constitution."

"Sure. I'll be right back."

"Jesus, Brad. You always have the same thing. Why do you always take time with the menu? You *always* eat the same exact thing." I tried to sound like I was teasing, but I was getting a little annoyed.

"Well, I might not this time. Christ, you ever see so many things on a menu in your life? What the hell is a Reuben sandwich? And look at the pictures. You think the food really looks like this?"

"Yes, exactly like that. A Reuben is a pastrami sandwich. On rye. With sauerkraut. You wouldn't like it. Just get the usual. Come on. We don't even have to pay for this meal, so live it up."

"So, have you folks decided?" I noticed that Debbie didn't have a pad to write our order down. I prefer it when they write down what you want so there's no mistakes.

"I'll have the salmon. With baked potato. Sour cream on the side."

"Mixed vegetables or salad?"

"Um. Is the salad mixed greens?"

"Ah, I don't think so. Tomato, cucumber, croutons."

"I think I'll have the vegetables."

"Vegetables, okay."

"Are they, what, steamed?"

"I think so. You want me to check?" I could tell Debbie didn't want to check.

"No, that's okay. Steamed is fine."

"And you, sir?"

"I don't know. Give me a sec."

"Okay. I'll come back again in a minute."

"No, no. Don't run off again. I'll have a cheeseburger, fries, onion rings on the side."

"And how would you like that cooked?"

"Medium. Medium rare, not medium well. Pink inside."

"Fine, sir." Debbie picked up the menus. She wasn't smiling now.

"I don't know. Nothing sounds that good to me. I don't like fast food that much."

"Wendy's is fast food. This isn't fast food." We have this argument all the time.

"I'm not in the mood for a burger is all I'm saying."

"So change your order. Have an omelet. You like eggs."

"Not for dinner. I don't like eggs for dinner. Besides there's the cholesterol. My triglycerides are way up."

"That's not eggs."

"Oh no? Then what is it?"

"I don't want to say. You'll get upset."

"No, I won't. I don't get upset Meg. Just spill it. What do you mean it isn't the eggs? What's that supposed to mean?"

"You're getting heavier. You don't exercise."

"Yeah, like that has anything to do with cholesterol. What, are you a doctor now?"

"I'm saying is all. Middle-aged men need to stay active."

"I'm not middle-aged."

"You're forty. What's that?"

"Forty isn't middle-aged. It's pre-middle-age. Fifty is middle age."

"Correct me if I'm wrong, but two times forty is eighty. You think eighty isn't approximately the average life span? Two times fifty is a hundred. How many hundred-year-olds do you know?"

"Middle doesn't mean half. Middle is the median age. Jesus. You really can be a pain."

"And fries? With onion rings? That doesn't sound like you're worried about triglycerides. Have fish. Fish has oils that are good for you. Fish oil. You can get it as a pill."

"Fish oil pills? You got to be kidding."

"I'm not. Janet takes them. Three a day."

"Janet from work?"

"Do we know another Janet? Yes, Janet. My co-worker."

"She's obese. What good's fish oil going to do her?"

"She is not obese. Her doctor prescribed it. Never mind. Really, it doesn't matter."

Brad shrugs and goes to the bathroom again. He's gone a long time, then I see that he's over in the bar watching the game on TV. This annoys me, but I don't say anything. After a while he comes back, rubbing his hands like he just washed them.

"So." Suddenly I don't feel like talking. Or even being there.

"Yeah?" Brad rips open a sugar packet and eats it.

"So. How was work?"

"It was terrible. God. It's crazy right now."

"What? What's going on?"

"We're all backed up. You know how many foreclosures we had this week? Just this week? I'm not talking about this month. Monday to Friday of this week."

"I know what a week is. What, ten?"

"Ten? You've got to be kidding. We had ten *yesterday*."

"Okay. Five million."

"Jesus."

"I'm kidding. Really, I have no idea."

"Twenty-seven. Twenty-seven people couldn't pay their mortgages for the past six months and we took their houses. Or will. The sheriff executes the writs, thank God for that. I don't want any part of it."

"That's a lot. A lot of families. Can't you let them stay?"

"Yeah, right. Meg, listen, we're a bank, not a charity. People get time. We give them six months, eight sometimes. And if they can pay a little we string it out longer. But we're a business."

"Still. I mean, that's like a hundred people, homeless."

"What's your point? They're not going to be living on the streets."

"How do you know that? I mean, if they can't pay for their house they sure as hell can't live in the Holiday Inn."

"With relatives. People have relatives."

"Do we?"

"Do we what?"

"Have relatives? In this town?"

"What are you saying?"

"I'm saying that not everyone has a place to go when First Federal kicks them out of their house. That's what I'm saying."

"Too bad. You have to pay. That's it. We work, we pay our bills. Some people are deadbeats. They buy too much house. They put in a pool, tennis courts. We had this guy crying in the office this week. I mean, literally crying. He had a quarter-mil note with us. A big house in the Heights. Pool, the works. You know what he did for a living? Guess?"

"He's an interpreter at the UN."

"Funny. He's a goddamned carpenter. A carpenter. What business does a carpenter have living up there? I mean, we couldn't live there. What does he expect?"

"That's kind of stupid. People can live where they want."

"Not if they can't afford it. You know what Rush says about the country, about the false hopes the Democrats encourage?"

"Hold that thought. Here's our food."

"All right then." It isn't Debbie who brings our food but some guy from the kitchen. His shirt is filthy. "Do you have the salmon?" The baked potato is covered in sour cream.

"And here, Sir, is your cheeseburger. Another Bud Light?"

"Yes please."

"Will you look at this? Jesus Christ." Brad pushed his plate away.

"What's wrong?"

GEORGE OVITT

"This burger. It's overcooked. And there's onions on it. Who wants onions?"

"Send it back."

"Right. And wait another half hour. I'll eat it."

"Here you are, Miss, and here's a refill on the waters. Anything else I can get you folks?"

"No."

"Nothing, thanks."

"What do you suppose happened to Debbie? This guy looks like he cooked the stuff. So where is she?"

"Beats me. On break probably."

"Look at this. Another fucking lemon. How hard is it to bring water without lemon in it? Did I ask for lemonade?"

"Brad, for Christ's sake, just eat. You've earned it, throwing all those people out on the street all week. Gives a person an appetite."

"Funny. Real funny. You think I like my job? I hate that bank. That asshole Craig."

"What about me? You think pushing paper is hard try standing on your feet cutting hair six hours a day."

"I don't push paper Meg. Not for like ten years."

"Whatever. So now you evict people electronically. Same dif."

"Boy, you're in a bad mood tonight."

This was the sort of thing Brad would say that made me crazy. But not tonight. So I just ate my salmon. It wasn't bad.

"How's the fries?" I had to say something. Brad was shoveling the fries into his mouth like there was no tomorrow.

"Edible. Want one?"

"Yeah, sure. Want to try the salmon? It's good."

"You know that I hate fish. The burger isn't that bad."

128

"So what did Rush say?"

"What?"

"You were saying, Rush said something. About the carpenter?"

"Oh yeah. Not about the carpenter. About how everybody feels entitled. That sack of shit Pelosi, Omama, the rest of them. They all promise the moon to your average jerk and get them to believe it. So they borrow money and buy a house they can't afford. And then I'm considered an asshole because I have to take it away from them. He said how when Reagan was in charge people didn't have the same sense of entitlement. Like they do now."

"And when did you hear this? Today?"

"On the way home from work. KZUN has a rerun at five."

"Lucky us. Well, I hate to break it to you Brad, but Rush is a creep."

"Right. Rush is the smartest man in America."

"Then we're in worse trouble than I thought."

"We're in trouble all right, but it's because of these liberals. Spending on everything. Christ, we owe the Chinese ten trillion dollars. How we supposed to pay them? Are we going to print a bunch of money?"

"How should I know? Ask Rush. I mean, the smartest man in America ought to know."

"That's funny, Meg. Rush didn't get us into this mess, or are you saying it isn't Obama's fault? Mr. Change-You-Can-Believe-In."

"As I remember it, it was your boy Bush who started the war. Am I right about that? I mean, was that particular war free? Did we get like a two-for-one deal on the Bush wars?"

"You know, Meg, sometimes I wonder about you. Do you honestly mean to say you don't see why we went to war against Sodom? He's sitting on half the oil in the world. A fricking dictator. We had to do it. What's-his-name even showed the pictures of the Iraq A-bomb, and those chemicals, that anthrax. You don't count the money you spend on war. It's this other stuff we do, free medical care, make-work jobs, social security. What kind of bullshit is that? I mean, if you can't buy your own insurance why should I have to pay for it?"

"Could you keep your voice down? People are looking at us."

Brad swiveled his head around and frowned at everyone within range.

"Brad, ask yourself this. Who's paying for that road out there? You? I mean, that's how it works. You chip in. And these people eating ribs and burgers and fish and chips, they chip in too. And we get a road. That's how it works. Rush is a creep. For him it's every man for himself, but he's rich so he can say that. We can't. I cut hair. That's what I do. Your wife cuts hair for seven bucks an hour plus tips. You think social security is a bad idea for somebody like me?"

"Number one, Meg, I pay for the road. Two, so what if Rush got rich? He sells something, we buy it. That's how America works. Three, I know what you do for a living. My job is to process paper on deadbeats. Maybe our jobs aren't so different. We're service people. It doesn't pay well, but it's honest work."

"Maybe. I'm not so sure. I work for Pimloco, Inc. Ever heard of it? Whoever the hell they are they own seventeen hundred shops—*seventeen hundred*. You know where the corporate office is located? You'll love this. In Shanghai. In China, Brad. I'm employed by a Chinese company to wash and set old ladies' hair here in Las Cruces." I thought I was going to cry.

"Welcome to America. Say hello to the twenty-first century."

"Fuck you Brad. I hate it when you patronize me."

Brad looked shocked. I never talk to him like this. I was dizzy with anger.

"Hey, slow down. This was a friendly disagreement, that's all. No need to get nasty."

"Hey Brad, why don't you go powder your nose or something? I want to drink my lousy Bud Light in peace."

He got up and walked into the bar.

I drank the beer and ordered another. It tasted like water, but it relaxed me a little.

After twenty minutes Brad came back to the table. He was wearing his contrite face.

I said, "I don't want to argue with you. You're conservative. I'm not a liberal, but I'm not like you. Let's leave it at that. It's Friday night. I'm too tired for this."

"So you give up?"

"Yes Brad. I surrender. You win. Is that what you want? Should I wave a white flag? Put up my hands?"

"That would be nice. How about just admit I'm right?"

"Even though I've forgotten what the argument was about, you're right. You're always right. And I'm wrong. Forever."

"Amen to that."

"You are such an asshole."

"Nice. A nice thing to say to me. Did I ever call you a name? Ever, in, what, sixteen years of marriage?"

"I don't remember. I can't remember this morning let alone sixteen years. Is it really that short a time? It seems like forever."

"Funny. It seems short to me because I love you."

"Really? And what does that mean? What does that mean to you? Does it involve listening to me sometimes, or taking my ideas seriously? Or just me listening to you?"

"Lighten up, Meg. I listen to you. We're just shooting the breeze here. I know I can get carried away sometimes."

"It's not that. It's not the disagreements. Look around. Remember what I said? This is the world, the real world. People laughing and eating and enjoying one another's company. I don't know much about the things you know about, but I do know that when someone gives you a gift—and I admit it isn't much of a gift, just a meal at Applebee's—you're obliged to enjoy it, to share it with the person you love."

"Yeah, you're right. I was being a prick. Sorry Meg, really."

"That's okay. Let's just eat and go home."

"Hey, Meg, look at me. Maybe I don't show it, but I do love you. Do you remember when we first met?"

"I remember."

"You were the best looking girl in that crappy high school. By far. Remember the prom. You had your hair up, so pretty."

"And you had no hair. Even then."

"Like my old man. At least I didn't comb it over."

"No. You were funny about it. The first shaved head I ever saw. It shone in the lights."

"And we made a nice couple. Didn't we? We had fun."

"Yeah, we did. We danced."

"That's not all we did."

"Um."

"So what happened? Where did we go wrong?"

"We didn't go wrong. We just went different. It happens."

"Different how?"

"You know. Every way you can."

"Maybe, maybe you're right."

I smiled a little. "Don't agree with me you dimwit. You're supposed to argue with me. You argue about everything else."

"Then we're alike. Hell, Meg, I don't know what we are, maybe tired, maybe worried like everyone else. You get old faster than you think is possible, you give up the dreams you had, you end up in a town that's just okay, eating in shitty places like Applebee's."

"It isn't shitty. This place is just fine. That's part of the problem with you. You won't *settle* for anything. Everyone takes things as they come. Not you though. Nothing's good enough for you."

"Except for you Meg. You're good enough for me."

"I'm too good for you."

"Yeah, you are." Brad had a nice smile. You forget how much someone's face can change when they smile.

"Ready to go?" I finished my third beer.

"You want any dessert?"

"Hm. Maybe. But not here."

"There's nothing at home."

I gave him my best leer—it wasn't much. "That's what you think."

"Really?" Brad smiled full bore.

"Yeah. Let's go home."

"Sounds good."

"If the check ever comes."

"Relax. She's a nice girl. She's doing her best."

"I suppose that's all we can ask."

"It's all we can ask."

Lost in Granada

"Huyendo del mal, de improvise/Se entra en el mal
Por la puerta del paraiso/artificial.
Fleeing from evil, unexpectedly/One enters evil
Through the door of a paradise/That is false."
Ruben Dario, *Poema del otono*, 1910

Deborah Watkins woke up with five different kinds of pain in her head.
There was dehydration—she refused to drink any but bottled water, and that
wasn't always available, and it was hot beyond belief, so dehydration was a
given. There was booze: she thought maybe rum and coke; yes, and coke too,
though perhaps not much of that; and sleeplessness dating back a month or
more—how long, Deborah asked herself, have I been here?—and then there
was some vague pain Deborah might have called moral or existential. Though
she had tried to avoid doing so, she had succumbed to a handsome but fatuous
minor actor who had tussled with her throughout a long and ultimately
ungratifying night. It had crossed her mind at some point that he was probably
acting, but then she remembered that he *couldn't* act, so she concluded that
he was unskilled in two areas. The brightness of the sun and the heat of the

morning did nothing to ease the ache in Deborah's head or heart. Perhaps she could sleep a bit more, but no, that was out of the question—she did have to go to work today.

And work, well that was also looking dismal. Everything had gone wrong with the shoot. Too many clouds or too few, all the wrong backgrounds—yes, it was a lovely city, but a little more run-down than the director wanted, full of ragged kids and slouching young men, insects, bad smells, dust and noise. The extras gawked at the camera. The unavailability of simple things like American cigarettes and American food made everyone testy. The cameramen were limp from the humidity and were unwilling to hang around for the nth take that the director needed either because he was a perfectionist or because he was incompetent.

And the script, well, that was no great shakes either. Deborah had come to see that the hero was a sadist and a puritan, incapable of joy, but joyfully violent. In yesterday's multiple takes, the Walker character—played by a handsome B-list actor who should have been doing shampoo ads—had ordered the execution of a 'legitimist' named Corral. Deborah, knowing that she had few skills as a judge of art, nonetheless thought the scene could have been powerful. The condemned man begged for mercy. Walker heard petitions to spare the former cabinet minister's life; the man's family tearfully begged the emotionally-distant leader of the filibusterers to spare their husband and father—but the sentence was carried out anyway, with Walker unmoved. Not bad. But the actual scene was full of bathos, overwrought, empty of feeling. Gareth, the director, had lectured the cast and crew on the 'allegorical' significance of Corral's execution. The poor man was to become a stand-in for all of Latin American history—he was Montezuma, Atahualpa, Bolivar, and Sandino wrapped into one—Gareth didn't know shit about any of this, but the writer had apparently been to the library and filled his script with pages of irrelevant and obscure facts. All bullshit, thought Deborah, nobody's going to get it.

Up. Deborah peeled her body from the damp sheets. The actor, luckily, had left many hours before—seeing him in her tiny bed would have been the last straw. The colonial-era hotel looked out over the town square and had full-length doors—no windows—that could be opened to let in the abundant, and blazing, sunshine. It was a nice hotel in some ways, but the palmetto bugs—Deborah thought they were actually cockroaches—were as big as her hand, and many of them, along with spiders, mosquitoes, and maybe lizards had been squashed over the years on the walls and ceiling, to such an extent that the entire airless room had the look of the inside of some abstract expressionist painting—Soutine maybe, but Deborah couldn't recall if he *was* an abstract expressionist. Things had gotten a little mixed up for her just lately. Never had she been in such an exotic place. Really, it was too much. And she refused to enter the shower under any circumstances. First, it was as mildewed as her parent's basement in Ohio; second, the hot water was supplied by running cold water over an exposed heating coil, with copper wiring that buzzed and glowed when you turned on the light switch. The thought of being electrocuted in the shower of a shabby hotel in Granada, Nicaragua, appealed to Deborah not at all. She washed up in the sink with water that smelled like Clorox.

Her face looked ghastly. She had sunburned and peeled twice—no amount of 30 or 45 kept the zapping x-rays from frying her fair hair and freckly skin. She'd be beef jerky after a couple of more weeks of this. Deborah was desperately thirsty but would not even consider the tap water. Perhaps there would be some bottled water available today in one of the town's tiny, under-stocked markets. Her clothes weren't in especially good shape either. She had never perspired so much in her life, and repeated washings in the sink had left her things sour-smelling and sticky. Nothing to do. She slipped into her cut-offs and a baggy tee shirt—no bra in this heat, despite the looks she got from the women and the possibly obscene suggestions made by a few of the younger men. Actually, although she didn't know a word of Spanish, Deborah felt as if most of the men and women in this small town were friendly. They ignored her and her co-workers, and no one had really hassled them, aside from a few aggressive beggars who hung around at the hotel. When she had been in Tijuana or Puerto Vallarta, Deborah had been whistled and hooted at from morning to night. One young Mexican had even walked right up to her on the street and grabbed her crotch like it was a cantaloupe. Deborah had been between boyfriends at the time, and her companion, a flakey unemployed actress named Janice, had laughed as if such a crude gesture was a joke. Anyway, Deborah found the men in Nicaragua more polite. The women, pretty when young and worn-out when older, stared at her more openly than the men did, and with more obvious disapproval. Deborah had decided a long time ago just to be herself, so she dressed and acted as she liked and expected everyone to deal with it.

She walked down the stairs to the lobby of the hotel, hoping not to see the actor—was it Ryan or Brian?—or anyone else from the crew. They were all there. Clusters of people were drinking coffee and discussing the day's filming. The weather was good, and Deborah, after grabbing a cup of coffee and avoiding eye contact with as many people as possible, joined the group of people with whom she felt most comfortable—electricians, carpenters, boom operators, and other techies.

"Deb, what's up? You look a little green," said Tom Nelson, the key grip.

"A long night. Anybody got any water?"

"Yeah, there's bottled water in the cooler."

Deborah drank deeply and immediately felt better. "So what's on the schedule for today?"

"Gareth says we have to reshoot the last scenes from yesterday. He looked at the dailies and didn't like the light at all," shrugged Tom, as if to say what do you expect?

"Well, whose fault is that?"

"Yours, you little bitch," Gareth was standing behind Deborah.

Deborah didn't care what Gareth thought. "Hey, you're the boss. If we have to do the scene again, fine."

The director looked into Deborah's eyes and said, "Snippy aren't we. I think I know why." And then, to the twenty or so technicians assembled in the hotel lobby, "All right people, time to get started. I want to go back over everything we did yesterday afternoon. The cast will be arriving at eight so let's get moving."

Deborah was annoyed that word of her indiscretion had already made its way to the director. Aside from being pompous and incompetent, Gareth was a gossip. No doubt he had told everyone within earshot that Deborah was sleeping around, so she could expect half a dozen unwanted come-ons before the day was over. Nothing for it. As she made her way to the vans that would take the crew to the *barrio* where they were filming, Deborah thought again that she had made a mistake signing on for this project.

Stuffed into the van with half a dozen of the crew, Deborah caught the gist of the conversation at once. It was an argument that had been going on nonstop for the past month.

"State of emergency my ass." This comment, from Ronnie Web, came in response to something Dale Fisher had said. Fisher was the only defender of Sandinista government on the crew. The rest of them, Deborah knew, were pissed off at being away from the States for so long.

"Hey Ronnie, there's a war going on here. What do you think's going to happen?"

"Christ, Dale, how stupid can you get? You think all this repression is about the war? Give me a break. A few farms were blown up and they shut down the press, arrest the opposition, shut down the Church. They're trying to force themselves on the country man, anybody can see that. Like fucking Castro. We're going to have to come in here and kick ass."

"Who's 'we' Ron? You going to join the Marines?"

"No, I'm not. 'We' is the good old US of A. As usual cleaning up the messes these people make."

"'The White Man's Burden,' right Ronnie?" said Dale. "Got to help these backward races get civilized? Man, I can't believe I'm hearing this in 1986. You forget about Vietnam already? Lebanon? Maybe you should read a newspaper."

Around it went. Deborah imagined that this argument would go on for eternity. Politics were pointless. Whoever shouted the loudest won the argument. She tuned out. As the van moved slowly through the narrow, badly paved streets, Deborah tried to look into the houses that sat on their edges. The children she saw were tiny—thin and cute. Their clothes were in tatters, and many of them had no shoes. She liked the way the houses were painted in bright pastel colors; sometimes she could imagine herself back in Mexico or even in some neighborhoods in LA, but most of the time she thought how strange Granada seemed, poor and yet pretty, harsh and irresistible. They rode past an old man riding an emaciated donkey. The man had a corncob pipe clutched in his teeth and a battered straw cowboy hat on his head. Tom, who was driving, slowed the van down to let the old man amble past. No one else on the crew seemed to notice, but Deborah wondered where the man was going or coming from. Maybe this was the story they should be telling in this movie. William Walker was a terrible person, a killer, a defender of slavery, so what was the point of glorifying him? Deborah still had a headache and her thoughts began to collide with one another. She shut her eyes. Sometimes it's best to tune everything out, she thought. But the place had a pull. It was terrible, but beautiful.

"I must be getting sick," she thought.

By noon, the sun was stripping the hair off of Deborah's head. She was full bore out in it, working the boom and trying to keep up with the rush of the action. The scene was exciting, in a predictable way. The actors—two dozen Americans and maybe fifty locals—were dressed in what was supposed to be nineteenth-century clothes. They had guns and were running around a lovely little whitewashed church shooting at one another. Deborah was bored, but she did her job. Anyway, who knew what the movie would look like when it was done? They might edit all this cartoonish violence into something worthwhile. But she doubted it. It also occurred to Deborah that what the writers and director were doing was making a surreal, mirror-image version of *High Noon*, complete with stoical anti-hero, grizzled bad-guys, and a cowardly populace. Too weird.

Nikki, whose last name Deborah had never caught, was helping with the boom and the sound gear, spelling Deborah as the filming went on longer and longer. At one point, as the rolling gun fight went into higher gear—the pantomime becoming a little hazy in the blasting heat—Nikki looked over at Deborah and rolled her eyes. A bit later, on break, she sat in the shade with Deborah to make small talk.

"Do you think they'll get the point?"

"Who?"

"Whoever the hell ever sees this. Okay. Lots of shooting. Violence and mayhem. Have we not shot four straight days of gun battles?"

141

"They won't use them all. Or maybe they will. I've lost track of what's going on here."

"It's barely a B thriller."

"No, I don't mean the movie. What I mean is, I've lost track of what's going on in general."

"Yeah, I hear you. Me too. I want to get out of here."

"I don't mean that either. I kind of like it here, sort of, in a weird way. Did you ever have that feeling that something was going on that you couldn't quite get, but it seemed important to figure it out?"

"All the time. When I'm stoned that's about how I feel about everything."

Deborah looked at Nikki and shook her head. "Forget it."

Nikki, a little pissed, asked Deborah in a not friendly way who she'd been sleeping with. "You made it with Brian right?"

"What are you talking about?" Deborah didn't like the question or the tone. Nikki was a skinny woman with big tits and dyed hair. Not someone Deborah would take any shit from.

"Or that yummy Mr. Walker?"

"That's bullshit times two. Who told you that?"

"Come on Deb," Deborah hated to be called Deb, and she figured Nikki knew it, "it's a small crew. Nobody has to make anything up. 'Sides, what else is there to do in this hellhole but screw around?"

"I think you're fishing here. You want to screw that dopey jock, be my guest." Deborah got up and walked across the plaza. The conversation had made her feel creepy. As she looked around at the cast and crew—everyone clustered in groups talking or eating—she thought of how alone she was in this place. She didn't have a friend, didn't know the language, and probably couldn't figure out how to get back to Managua by herself. The thin layer of friendliness that sometimes exists at the beginning of a location had evaporated, leaving everyone on edge. The whole scene felt desperate rather than congenial.

She walked up to Tom. He was brittle but good-natured. "Hey Tom, I'm feeling pretty sick to my stomach—you know, the water. Can you give the boom to Nikki? I need to get back to the hotel."

"We told you not to drink the water Deborah. Yeah, go ahead. But no one can drive you back; you're going to have to walk. Can you make it?"

"Hope so. I mean, what the hell Tom, if I die in the streets maybe you could stop and load my body in the van."

"Not my fault. Gareth wants the vans here in case we decide to shoot somewhere else. Sorry."

Deborah didn't really care. Right now she wanted to be left alone. "Sure, whatever. See you tonight at dinner."

"Get better."

Deborah waved and started to walk back to the center of town. She knew the way, if only vaguely. It struck her as strange that no street had a name, no house a number. When people told you where to meet them they referred to landmarks like 'the dying acacia tree,' or 'the house with the blue door.' Anyway, what the hell, she felt worn out and needed to be alone.

The streets were hot and dusty. Not crowded, but not empty. The smells that rose up in the stifling air were sweet and putrid: the aroma of corn, earthy and acrid; the smell of frying meat, of dampness, rot, and sewage. Large-tailed black birds, grackles Deborah had been told, cackled and screeched in an unnerving way as they scuttled from trees to the ground, picking at whatever waste was lying in the gutters—apparently no one used trash cans in this city, or anyplace else in Nicaragua for that matter.

On the second corner that Deborah passed there was a little café—a couple of tables perched on the edge of the street, a Fanta sign out front, a few people inside. Deborah, without thinking, walked through the open door and went up to the counter. A woman was leaning on her elbows, reading a newspaper. Deborah remembered somebody telling her that '*hay*' worked in nearly every situation. So, pointing at the sign for drinks, Deborah tried "*Hay rum y Coca-Cola?*" To her surprise and delight the woman smiled, nodded her head in the affirmative, and held up one finger. "Yes, *si'*" said Deborah. Not bad at all. A few minutes later she was sitting in one of the chairs on the edge of the sidewalk sipping a lukewarm rum and coke, feeling as if she had just surmounted a vast cultural crevasse. Is it really this easy? If I had wanted a steak and a beer, I could have gotten them.

As she sipped the sickeningly sweet drink Deborah felt plugged into the scene, but also strangely detached from herself—could she still be fucked up from last night? The people on the street, the harsh light, the buildings, all had a slightly unreal feel to them. A small group of soldiers walked up the street. Their guns looked enormous to Deborah. The men were young and good looking. They looked at Deborah, and she was pleased to see that they wouldn't hold her eyes. She still had the power. Deborah saw herself as a sophisticate, as a chick who had done it all, but she'd never done a guy from another country. Maybe once—a Canadian, if he really was one, but she'd been drunk and partying and didn't really remember. Deborah swilled down the rest of her rum and coke. How, she wondered, had she become so trippy? The soldiers were gone up the street now, joking and laughing in their incomprehensible way, but Deborah wanted to imagine that they were talking about her. She knew she looked good, in a beat-up, sunburned *gringa* way. Deborah had never understood the whole feminist thing, to be honest. She liked it when guys looked her over. She liked the chase and, once in a while, giving in. Then, mostly, what followed sucked since every one of the men she'd ever been with didn't have a clue about her. Like that dimwit last night; Deborah hadn't gotten into it at all. To tell the truth, half the time men bored her. Deborah, who was—she had to admit—just a little too dizzy, a little too detached, closed her eyes and drifted in the hot afternoon. She wished she had a joint or some coke. That would be just the thing. Level things out, blunt the edges. Kind of an exotic scene when you came down to it. People were walking by and no one noticed her; she was fading out, dimming into the heavy air and reddening sun. And that was fine too.

More time passed. Deborah lost track of its passing. She might have nodded off for a few minutes. There might have been some dreaming—who could say? When she was paying attention again, Deborah noticed that the streets were now deserted. The sun was angling downward, fading out, leaving an eerie stillness over the town. Her drink was long gone; there was a brown, sugary scum etched into the glass. Deborah's stomach started doing a dance. She wasn't at all sure how things had gotten this bad. She held her legs tightly together, closed her eyes, tried to think about home, but that went nowhere. The spasms passed, but Deborah knew if she sat still she was going to be sick. She got up and started to walk as fast as she could in what she thought was the direction of the hotel. Trouble was she had no idea where she was going. Downhill was easier, so she walked that way, turning from one street into another. Like anyone who is lost, Deborah kept thinking that there, just around the corner, was her destination, but when she turned the corner there was just another street of identical, unrecognizable houses. The streets gradually narrowed, as if they were a funnel leading Deborah into some great void. The *barrio* she was walking through was seedy. Her mother had always warned Deborah never to walk alone in a strange city. Deborah cringed at the memory of her mother's voice. She mumbled "help me please" to herself, hoping the magic of her usual luck still held. Even though she held her head up and looked like someone going someplace nearby, she had no idea where the hotel might be, or where she was, or how she was going to get out of this maze of streets. There were a few men leaning on the buildings. They looked her over; some laughed or spoke to her in words that seemed both to caress and violate her. Another street, another turn, another row of run-down houses and shops. The grackles screamed at her. Deborah's head was pounding and she began to weep.

More men. Nothing she could do—she kept walking, faster. As she approached the group, one of the men, young and tall, walked toward Deborah and stood in front of her. She tried to walk around him; he took hold of her arm, not roughly, but firmly. He was speaking to her rapidly, pointing to the house across the street, a tiny filthy-looking shack with cracked windows and peeling white paint. Deborah tried to pull away, but the young man held her arm and steered her toward the open door. One of the other men yelled something at them. Deborah was terrified. She felt her stomach begin to give way. The man pushed her inside the house.

It was dark and cool in the room. The house was bigger than it looked from outside—neater, cleaner. There was a big table, and at the table a family—an old woman, an old man, a middle-aged couple, half a dozen children. There was food on the table, a white tablecloth, dishes, pitchers, candles. The room was close but it smelled good, like a holiday at home, like Thanksgiving, a holiday Deborah barely remembered. As the young man led Deborah into the room, the middle-aged woman stood up and smiled at her. One of the children got up from the table and guided Deborah, who was weeping, to a seat on the bench. Everyone smiled at her. Deborah tried to smile back, but her face felt paralyzed. Still, the family smiled. Then, as one, every person at the table reached out and took the hand of the person sitting next to them.

The children on either side of Deborah took her hands in theirs—tiny hands that were soft and comforting—and the old man seated at the head of the table began to say words that seemed to Deborah to mean something she had once known but had long ago forgotten. The family members closed their eyes and spoke in a whisper, together, as one person. The words rose above the table, up toward the smoke-darkened ceiling, out the open door, and into the darkening streets. The words wrapped around the surrounding houses and fell into rooms full of neighboring families as they sat and spoke their own words. The *barrio* seemed to float on the words, on the prayers of the families that held one another's hands in little circles. The children felt happy saying the words that their mothers had taught them, and the mothers and fathers felt the warm hands of their children to be, at that moment, the point of their lives. Then the moment passed, and everyone opened his eyes, and the smiles returned to each face, and the hands took up the thick tortillas, food was passed and shared and eaten. The children laughed and shyly touched the light, sun-flecked skin of the *Norteamerica*, the pretty stranger whose eyes were damp but whose face was easing into quiet happiness.

Deborah knew that she hadn't been lost at all. She had been coming to this room all along. Now, she thought, she was home, although she wasn't sure what that meant.

Anyway, it didn't matter. Just then, it didn't matter at all. She ate and laughed and spoke a language she didn't know, and everyone seemed to understand. And that, for the moment, was enough.

In the End, What We Love is Ourselves

There's a woman. She is lonely. She loves reading, especially poetry. When she can, she goes to poetry readings, falling in love with the words and images, and sometimes, in the way real readers do, with the poets themselves.

One day she's in a bookstore downtown, one of the used bookstores in Society Hill. She picks up a book of poems by a poet she adores. The poet's name was Alberto Blanco, a Mexican poet, but that isn't important. In fact, it probably wasn't Alberto Blanco at all; I think I was recently reading *El Corazón del instante* so I supplied that name. The woman opens the book to see how much it costs, and inside, written on the fly leaf, are the words "This book belongs to A. If you should find it, please call . . . ." and there's a phone number from someplace far away—it turns out to be Mexico City. So the woman—let's call her Jane—purchases the book—it's very expensive, a rare and coveted volume, but she must own it—and when she gets home she reads through the poems several times. They move her deeply. The writing is sensuous, insightful. They are in Spanish; they remind Jane of Pablo Neruda, whom she adores, or of Roberto Bolaño, a poet she has only recently read. Someone who would own this book is someone she would like to meet. And over the next couple of weeks, this woman, who is pretty and sad and alone, concocts an elaborate fantasy about calling the book's owner. She thinks of how they will speak on the phone and discover that they both love the same writers. He will adore Cortázar as much as she does, and will have memorized Lorca's *Gypsy Ballads*. But, of course, this notion is absurd. Young women don't phone unknown men in hopes of reciting ballads long distance. What could such a call accomplish?

Of course, she calls. There is much jangling and buzzing on the phone line. Eventually, a man answers. It hadn't occurred to the woman that the owner of the book would be female. Why not? She felt it. The handwriting on the flyleaf was self-assured, masculine. Nor did Jane think the person who wrote the words would be dead—surely that was possible?—no, it wasn't possible. Now, on the phone, the man's voice is strong and expressive. Jane's Spanish, which is quite good, is up to the task of a phone conversation. Things are going well. Jane blurts out the facts: she has the book, the message, she wasn't sure, but she herself knows how much certain books mean to their owners. What wonderful poems they are! How lovely and full of passion! And, to her delight, the man on the other end of the line is kind, grateful for her thoughtfulness, for the call. Yes, the book was precious to him. He was forced to sell it during a difficult period. He was divorcing his first, his only, wife. Money was in short supply. Books were sold, paintings, records. It was terribly painful. She understands. She has never been married, never divorced, but she has sold things that she treasured. It is like amputating an arm. She babbles now; admittedly she is not herself. The man introduces himself. He is, indeed, named Alberto, but his last name is something else—it is Cerro. Yes, having that book would mean a great deal, memories from happier days, but he couldn't, no, it would be an imposition. She insists. She would love to do something, a gesture. The past is all we have. They discuss the matter.

Mailing the book doesn't come up. Somehow, at this point, it is clear that they will meet. She cannot believe her luck. He insists on a face to face meeting. He must know this kind woman. Perhaps he might bring her a book of his own, one that he has written. He is a writer? Yes, one of modest renown in Mexico, not well known, translated, but poorly. Though his English, she notes, is flawless, much better than her Spanish. They agree to meet. He will be in Austin, Texas, in a month. He is, it turns out, an academic. Better and better. He will be presenting a talk at the University on the younger Mexican poets, on Veronica Volkow and Manuel Ulacia, on Pedro Serrano and Francisco Segovia. Has she read them? No? Well perhaps something can be done. A gesture, for he too is fond of them. And so a plan is made. They will meet in Austin in March. She can arrange to do something professional; perhaps Jane is a librarian or a professor herself. Or involved in theatre. Or perhaps she has never visited Texas—many people haven't—and would like to see the scenery. An opportunity. Kill two birds. *Matar dos pájaros*. It is settled. At the hotel. In the bar. Six p.m., March something or other. We needn't dwell on logistics.

The woman is beside herself with anxiety, joy, eager anticipation. A mature man, a scholar, a lover of poems. Mexican. What will he be like? She shops for a new dress, but is embarrassed to have done so; nonetheless, she packs it. Indeed, she packs her little suitcase a week before her departure. She passes several sleepless nights, has erotic dreams, which isn't unusual, but now there is an identifiable man in them—tall, graying, distinguished. At last the day comes. She flies to Dallas or Houston, some god-forsaken city whose airport is larger than New Jersey. Takes a second plane, a tiny two-engine prop plane that bounces in the rough air of the Great Desert. Not an eager flier, the woman is nonetheless indifferent to the rough air—she herself is afloat on a great sea of yearning. She lands in Austin. Takes a taxi, surprisingly expensive, to the hotel, the Hilton as it turns out. Checks into an expensive suite, the only room that was available. More than she can afford, but she can afford nothing, so what difference does it make? No one quibbles about money in such circumstances. She showers and dresses. Something modest, but with a hint of sensuality. She is, after all, a lovely woman. In fact, she is a beautiful woman, whose loneliness is really inexplicable, and yet there are many lonely women who are beautiful. She prepares herself, all the while thinking about the love poetry of Neruda, the songs of desire and loss that have moved her since she was a girl. Carefully, slowly, she dresses, combs her long brown hair, applies her make-up—just a dab of eye shadow, lipstick. A deep breath.

At five minutes before six o'clock she walks into the hotel bar. No one is there. She sits down at the bar. She wonders whether to order a drink or not. Perhaps the man dislikes women who drink. Many thoughts circle through one's mind in such moments. She decides to order white wine, which she dislikes, but its neutrality seems to her to strike just the right note. White wine isn't a drink but an accessory, an affectation.

At ten minutes past six o'clock a man walks into the bar. He is carrying a tan briefcase—she remembers this detail afterward—and a stick. The stick is white with a red tip: the universal sign of legal blindness. The man reaches awkwardly for the bar. The bartender goes to him; words are exchanged; the bartender points in the direction of the woman—she is the only person he could point to—then, realizing his mistake, the barman reaches over the rail of the oaken bar and takes the arm of the blind poet and scholar and guides him toward the woman. The Mexican man, Alberto Cerro, taps at the stools with his cane and takes the kind of shuffling steps that unsighted people take in strange rooms. He is indeed tall, gray, middle-aged, distinguished. His face is somewhat marred by empty eye sockets. He does not wear dark glasses, and he stares off to the side, following perhaps the slight cues of sound provided by his better senses, but the effect is of a man who is off balance, ready to topple at any moment onto the burgundy carpet. He arrives at the woman's side. She gets up and introduces herself. He reaches his hand out toward her. She hesitates and then takes it. His hand is surprisingly soft, moist. He scuttles onto a stool and orders an Old Fashioned. The woman feels—what? Disappointed to be sure, but then also disappointment in herself—what did she expect? She realizes now that the man might have been gay, or obese, or a serial killer. He is merely blind. But he is still the man who owned the lovely book of poems, who spoke thoughtfully to her over the phone, who is a professor at the Mexican Autonomous University, who is here to read a paper, written, it transpires, in Braille, to the Comparative Literature Department of a major American university.

They begin to chat. She orders another glass of wine, red this time. He is charming in person. Gradually the woman is able to look at Alberto's face. He isn't bad looking, only disfigured. He speaks directly to her. He apologizes for not mentioning his "infirmary"—that is precisely the word that he uses— and he apologizes also for his "clumsy English," though his command of English is as good as the woman's; he uses the subjunctive perfectly. They discuss poets whom they admire as well as Marquez and Vargas Llosa and the great Bolaño—she is well read in Latin American literature, especially since she has crammed for her date. The *charla*—he calls it that at one point—is a delight for both of them. After an hour or so, he excuses himself. He has to appear at the University early in the morning, he is tired from his long flight. They shake hands again. He leans forward and, awkwardly, but with a gallantry she is unfamiliar with, and kisses her cheek. He walks again with the strained gait of the blind toward the elevator. She realizes that she might have offered to take him upstairs, but that such an offer might have been misconstrued.

She has naturally forgotten to give Alberto his book—it is still packed in her suitcase upstairs. What folly! She has another glass of wine—her third or fourth—and, her own gait somewhat constrained by alcohol, retires to her room where she proceeds to fall deeply asleep.

In the morning Jane attempts to phone Alberto's room so that she can return the book. He has checked out hours before. She phones the University and after much waiting and reconnecting is put through to the Comparative Literature Department. The talk is just ending. It is, the woman discovers to her horror, nearly eleven o'clock. The secretary promises to try and deliver a message to the guest speaker, to Alberto Cerro, but she cannot promise that she will have an opportunity. Of course, the woman must check out of the over-priced room. Checking out takes forever. She calls a cab, and finally is driven to the University. She arrives too late. Or not. In any case, the blind scholar from Mexico is nowhere to be found on the city-sized campus.

Jane is disappointed, but also strangely relieved. She cannot sort out her feelings properly. Somehow though, over the course of past twenty-four hours, she has discovered a previously hidden and unattractive part of her personality. Who is she really? A woman who flies halfway across the country to meet a strange man? A woman who is vain, hungry for love or, at least, companionship? Someone whose romantic inclinations cloud her judgment? Or, is she like the rest of us—alone, yearning for something? But then, when that thing appears, or when it might have been conjured up from the ordinary circumstances of life, the way all of the things worth having are ultimately conjured up, she is disappointed. In the end, Jane is happy to go home, to return to her apartment and her job and the life she felt to be so confining. She is, she decides, a person who is content to be alone and who, in the end, loves only herself.

Months pass. She forgets about the book. It remains on her shelf, unread.

The Invisible Fish

An oddball cross section of my family—a brother, a sister, an uncle, two aunts, a nephew and a niece—came to meet me at the airport. They came, I knew, not out of a sense of duty or affection but out of curiosity. They came to gawk, or maybe to see if, like the lowering clouds of January, I'd produce hail or lightening. The mid-morning sun was barely visible, and Tampa smelled like damp palms. It was too cool for Florida. Since I hadn't prepared a speech for the unexpected crowd I just said that I wished it were warmer.

"No way," said my Uncle Toby. "We love it, love it cool. Don't we all love the cool weather?" My Uncle is an immense, flabby man, florid and unhealthy, who had been the first to get out of New Jersey, first to buy a condo in St. Pete, the first to make a killing in the booming area of geriatric health care.

"Love the cool weather," my Aunt Doris confirmed, hugging me and getting her sullen teenage son to take my carry-on bag. Ralph was of some indeterminate adolescent age, and I had never seen him without his boom box and Gators hat. He was listening to some crappy song by Pink Floyd.

"That's okay, Ralph. I got it." But he couldn't hear me, or wasn't listening, and grabbed my bag with its gifts and magazines and medicine. Listening isn't big in my family; they're talkers, eager to impart news, mostly about money made and spent or awaiting spending—a kind of corporate entity unto themselves, wheeling and dealing from morning to night.

"I hate warm weather." This pronouncement came from my big brother Don, the slickest of the group, just forty, dressed, as usual, in a five-hundred dollar suit, wearing, of all things, a white fedora and looking like what he was, a crooked lawyer. He'd made his first real money defending Raytheon against the "frivolous lawsuits" brought by New Jersey homeowners who'd taken issue with the company for its dumping of cadmium and lead into their groundwater. Don's a big believer in corporate rights, a crusader against the "fucking *vox pop*" as he puts it. He thinks of himself as one of the good guys, the unappreciated toilers-in-the-trenches of capitalism who keep the wheels of commerce turning. Of course, all his good deeds are well rewarded—like Toby, he's a rich man. He's also been indicted for insider trading, which is why he's living in a hick town like St. Petersburg. Even though he got off, Don thought it wise to cool his heels for a few years on the Gulf Coast. That way he could keep an eye on the family money, ingratiate himself with our mother, and live the good life.

"Let's get a picture, a group shot!" Aunt Barbara is married to my younger brother, Top. She's a slender, emaciated blond whose fondness for diet pills has made her as brittle as glass. She started jostling everyone into tight group for a photograph, but nobody cooperated.

"How's Top doing?" I asked. My other brother wasn't there because he was off on one of his periodic "business trips," doing a stint of rehab or shacked up over on the East coast with some bimbo.

"Working, he's working. You know Top."

"All too well."

"Let's go, come on people, Mom's waiting for us." My sister Rita was always worrying about Mom, whose displeasure bubbled over at a moment's notice.

Toby took a picture. It slid out of the Polaroid yellow and faded, as if it were of the past.

We piled into station wagons for the trip to the beach. Don drove a Caddy and preferred his own company. I got in the back of Doris's Ford with my niece Cally, a precocious ten-year-old. She was reading a Nancy Drew book and paid no attention to me.

My mother had moved from North Jersey to the Gulf Coast when my father had his tax problems and, soon afterwards, his cancer. Since Pop died the family had been more or less getting along—the resentments that bound us together were festering beneath a thin surface of alleged concern for Mom and astonishment that the Old Man wasn't around to bully us. He had been one of those men who appear ageless, preserved by their bitter struggle against the rest of the world. Pop had devoted himself to becoming rich, and then powerful, and then immortal. He made money in real estate in New Jersey, betting on the development of the far western suburbs long before they were anything but pristine oak and pine woods. Then he parlayed his development money into the first big shopping center in Maplewood, at one time a rustic weekend retreat for New Yorkers and now a depressing, overbuilt bedroom community that fed its residents onto the clotted highways leading to Newark and the Lincoln Tunnel. After he made a million dollars—it was more than that, but he always referred to himself as a "simple millionaire,"—he involved himself in local Republican politics, moving from the Somerset County Board to the chairmanship of the North Jersey Republicans. He chaired Nixon's campaign in 1960 and Goldwater's in '64. The following year he became the mayor of Bernardsville. Union labor was abundant in North Jersey—carpenters, masons, and electricians all worked in closed shops—so shop stewards and union bosses could squeeze the big contractors anytime just by pulling one subcontractor off a job. Pop hated unions, but he understood how greed functions in the free market. He set up a "trust fund" which was basically a pot of unreported contributions from the biggest contractors in North Jersey, and he used the funds to buy Christmas gifts for the heads of the various trade unions—season tickets to the Giants or Rangers, mid-winter vacations to Miami, watches and scotch and cigarettes handed out by his supporters on the Fourth of July and Labor Day—and pretty soon all the local labor trouble vanished. Not too long after that—it was the late '60's—a politician just as ambitious and just as corrupt as my old man, a Democrat named Bert Mattoli, started an investigation of procurement policies in the county. It didn't take long to find enough dirt on the Mayor to get an indictment. Pop wasn't a cautious man; he'd always felt invincible, especially since he'd come through the Good War unscathed. That bit of good luck wasn't Pop's doing but a by-product of his own father's influence in the War Department. Grandpa Jack had been a college buddy of Stimson's, and Grandpa had seen to it that his son spent the war working on General Marshall's staff, a glorified clerk who made major without hearing a shot fired. Favors breed favors like money breeds money. "It's sweet to earn a buck, but sweeter to let money earn itself," was something Pop believed with his whole heart. And: "It isn't what you know but who you know." The folk wisdom of the immoral. The really big thieves don't bother with folksy sayings—they just steal a lot and disappear. Or run for president. But Pop wasn't all that bright. He was snazzy and glib and thought nobody could touch him. He took chances and got snared by a schmuck he despised—"a fat wop with a bad haircut." He didn't go to jail—nobody in New Jersey goes to jail for corruption—but he did have to step down as mayor and that, combined with being voted out of the Short Hills Country Club and off the rolls of the Optimists, was enough to kill him.

The airport at Newark where I had boarded my flight earlier that morning was a simple, low-lying, rather shabby building surrounded by 707's—Eastern and Delta and National—a bunker that had been weather-worn to a pasty gray. If you were boarding a plane you walked across the tarmac and climbed up a set of rollaway stairs into the smile of a young woman who seemed happy to see you, as if you were a relative arriving home for the holidays. Welcome aboard. The air blasting through nozzles wasn't fresh but overlaid with disinfectant; a peek into the cockpit with its instruments, too many, suggesting how complicated flying a plane really was and how much could go wrong. Buckled in, flipping through the in-flight magazine, with its happy couples—young, trim, sexy—floating in transparent blue-green water or lying on an otherwise empty beach, some Caribbean island served by Eastern, someplace where I might go and drink rum concoctions and forget my troubles. But of course your troubles fly with you, right through take-off and the warmed over pepper steak and scalding coffee, your troubles float around you like the billowy cumulus clouds that you can never quite believe won't crush the plane with their apparent solidity. The strange illusions of modern life: that the cities below are tidy and unpeopled; that the landscape is unmarred and flows along smooth topographical maps toward rivers whose every curve you can trace, from high country to the great watersheds of the Delaware and the Santee. The illusion that moving five miles above the earth at five hundred miles an hour is a simple matter of lift and thrust—incomprehensible to be peering down at the Atlantic Coast, at the barrier islands whose lines appear to mesh perfectly with the bending of the coast. It's so reasonable up here. The world is just as it should be, created to suit us, with our aches and longings. For a moment I imagine myself falling out of the sky, into the distant water, and then, miraculously, swimming ashore, into the arms of a beautiful woman who adores me.

And then I arrive and everything is just as it was the last time. Only worse.

In the car with my cousin and aunts I'm just another tourist, looking out the window at the whitecaps on Tampa Bay, brown pelicans diving into the waves and shitting on the pilings, a dead forest of guano-stained poles jutting out from the long causeway that links Tampa to St. Pete and the other Gulf beaches. Sometimes you saw a dolphin, or a porpoise—I don't know the difference—just off the bridge.

I like the water. Just looking at it makes me feel better.

Across the bridge, the long stretch north past the garbage dump, gulls swirling above the two lane road with bits of offal in their bills, past the cemetery where Mom wants to "rest," as she puts it, right there, under the tupelo trees hung with gray-black Spanish Moss, like sad old women. Everyone in my family owns a plot in there. Not me. This ground will be underwater someday and the coffins will rise out of the sandy ground and float out into the Bay. Turning east on Fifth Street, land as flat as land can be, tiny run-down cottages, black sand and patchy grass, mangy dogs on chains, strip malls, one after another. I know this piece of the town by heart. The big molar outside Dr. Grasso's office across from the Florida Power Building with its flooded green lawn; Haslet's Bookstore on 22nd, the Cuban sandwich place I like, more bungalows and palms and no people in sight. Cars, but no people—that's Florida.

And then we're there. I could see the Gulf out to the west, and our little caravan buzzed down the beach road to Mom's condo, twenty feet from the oat grass and rolling sand of the peninsula. It's pretty. The Gulf of Mexico is flat as a lake. No waves, just little absent-minded curls of white foam that seem too timid to push more than a few feet up the blindingly white sand. Like a picture you might see in one of the L-shaped Motels that line the beach—the Lido, the Palms, and of course the Sandpiper. Ten-unit Mom and Pop places too modest for my family. Before they bought condos and houses we'd stay in the over-priced Holiday Inn with its rotating eighth-floor restaurant.

Mom's condo is high class. 'A community for older adults' was carved into the driftwood sign at the gate; the 'community' consisted of a recreation center where bingo and bridge amuse a few blue hairs, and an over-chlorinated pool nobody ever uses. It turns out old people stick close to their television sets. If you walk around the place at night all you can see is the glow of flickering lights and the echoing of canned laughter. Mom never goes out. Toby sends one of his kids to check on her once a week, and Doris takes her to the Acme every Saturday morning for her frozen entrees, English muffins, tea and cigarettes. And gin. Mom's a prodigious drinker. Gin and tonics are her afternoon beverage, though she likes a nip or two straight up with lunch and a martini or three before her microwaved dinner. Otherwise she watches TV and works on cheap books of anagrams and word puzzles. Pop had stashed her in the condo so he could go back to New Jersey and screw his secretary—not literally his secretary, but some employee of the town or county who probably hoped the old man would set her up in a tenured state job. Which he did. Giving some broad a job would have been small potatoes for Pop. So Mom got stuck in Florida and turned out to like it. Then, one by one, a few of her relatives and a few of Pop's decided to make the move down here to get away from legal problems or to make a killing in real estate or some other unproductive form of work. The whole story is incredibly sickening. Florida is like a lot of places in America—if you aren't an idiot, and don't set too many moral impediments in the way, you can get rich. What else matters?

Mom pretended to be glad to see me. Big hug, how was I? Mom can be okay. How was New Jersey, my job? Mom never looked at you when she talked. Never took the cigarette out of her mouth except for that little dry peck on the cheek—European kisses she called them. The TV was on, blasting a soap, the window shades drawn against the light, the room a fog of nicotine. Some of the family paid their respects and then left for work or the mall or wherever.

Don, who thought of himself as the head of the clan, and Gillian, my oldest sister, who hadn't bothered to come to the airport, started in on me right away. We had lunch and a few drinks, and then went for a walk on the beach while Mom took a nap. Mom was slurring her words by mid-afternoon. She would sleep awhile then get up in time for cocktails. It was a family ritual. Don or somebody else would suggest she lie down. The younger cousins would take over the television. The women, my aunts, would do the dishes and smoke and gossip. Ours is a patrician family, without sophistication—if we'd lived in the old days, Pop would have had slaves and a bunch of mulatto kids. Don would have been the overseer, whipping the field hands. Toby would have run the plantation and counted the money. Gillian, my sister, would have been Scarlett O'Hara, but sluttier. We're from New Jersey, so our corruptions are run-of-the-mill—we're small-town crooks.

"So what's up with you little brother?" Don calls me this, or LB, knowing I hate it.

"Nothing much Don."

"Come on little guy. What are you up to? Getting laid?" Don put a thick arm over my shoulders. I shrugged it off.

"Just trying to find a job."

"Not trying too hard," said Gillian.

"What's that supposed to mean?" I knew what it meant, but you have to fight back.

"What I said. You're not looking too hard because, last we heard, you didn't have one."

Gillian is a beautiful woman; she breaks men's hearts. She's tall and slender and has long blond hair. Wears scanty clothing, or if she dresses up, manages to look undressed. Blue eyes, full of death.

"How would you know Gil? You been up to visit me? You called? Not since I got out of the hospital. So I'm pretty sure you don't know what I've been doing."

I hadn't been in the hospital, but it sounded good.

"You haven't been in the hospital," Don said. "Don't start in with the bullshit LB. We know what you've been up to."

"So why do ask me? You know everything, why ask?"

"You've been taking Mom's money, we know that," says Don.

"She gives me money. She doesn't mind. At least I've never heard her complain."

Don sighed. Gillian took my arm. We were walking on the beach, a long empty stretch of sand on the Gulf of Mexico.

"LB, you know better than that. Mom never complains. Look, you went to college, and still you've fucked up every job you ever had. You married the wrong woman, got involved with her nutty family. Luckily no kids, but still, alimony. You had a crappy lawyer and you didn't let us help you get out cheap. Can you see why we might be worried? Nobody begrudges you a chance, but, shit little brother, you've had them. So what Gillian and I want from you is a plan. A set of goals. Some idea of how you're going to get from A to Z."

"A to Z. What does that mean? What the hell is Z?"

"Z is out of our hair. On your own, supporting yourself," said Gillian.

"How about if I go to like, R?"

"Funny. No LB, all the way to fucking Z."

"Or what?"

Don pointed his finger in my face. He liked that, pointing, pushing.

"Or your allowance ends."

"I don't think so Don."

"And why not little brother? Why the fuck not?"

"Because I happen to know a few things about you and Toby. Not things you'd want anybody at your club to know."

"What club you talking about?"

"I don't know, don't all you gangsters belong to a club? Golf, tennis, cards? You blackmail me and I'll do the same to you."

"I can't believe you're threatening me. You don't know anything about my business."

"You think? Who do figure the Old Man confided in when he was up North? Or Mom? You think I'm stupid, but I'm not stupid. I could take you down."

"Take me down"? Don laughed until he started coughing. He spit out a wad of phlegm on the white sand. "Take me down, that's real good little brother, real good. You a fed? I'll take your ass down right now." Don wasn't a fighter, but he squared off in front of me. I wasn't a fighter either.

"All I'm saying is you can't cut me off. Look at me. I can hardly walk." My knee did hurt just then. Arthritis runs in the family.

"That's too bad."

"Okay. See what I do to you. And you too Gil."

Gillian slapped me, hard.

"I'll get you both." I was trying not to cry.

"Brother, you're full of crap. You think you can drag me down for some penny-ante bullshit business deal? I beat the IRS already, twice. You're dumber than I thought."

Gillian stepped up to hit me again. I put up my hands. She pushed against my leg. It didn't hurt, but it could have. She's strong, a street fighter.

"Jeez Gil, cut it out."

Gillian laughed at me.

Don stomped around. Gillian leaned into me. I could smell her perfume. After a beat she backed away.

"Okay, enough," said Don.

Gillian backed up. She knew when to defer.

"Look LB, we know you've been through a lot."

"I take it that you're divorced, I mean, legally?" Gillian asked.

"Is there any other way?"

"Excuse me Tommy, but didn't you marry a woman once before and then marry another one bigamously? You know, like two wives at once?"

"That was a long time ago. And that wedding in Mexico wasn't legal. So, no, I'm not married to anyone, and I'll be damned if I plan to be again."

Don said, "Probably best for all."

I let that go.

Gillian put her long nail into my chest and said, "A to Z baby. I want to hear what you've got to say."

"All right. You want a plan from me? My plan is to get out of here, go back to New Jersey and get a job. Real estate maybe, or use my accounting degree."

"Don can make some calls, maybe."

"That'd be good."

"And where you going to live?"

"In the house, where I've been living."

"No way LB. We're selling that property. The family needs the cash and the house is too big for you."

"But it's my house."

"The hell it is. You never paid a cent for it. No. You can take a few weeks to find something else, and I'm sure Mom will front you the money you need to move, but we want you out of there by summer."

I hadn't counted on this. I knew I wouldn't be able to get a job. The house was what I had.

"You two are bastards, you know that?"

"Hey Little Brother, watch your mouth. We mean what we say. You've been a pain in the ass, and it's got to stop."

"And how's that cow you married, what's her face?"

"You know her name Gil. Her name was Lillian. Is. Don't talk about her like that."

Gillian laughed again. "She's a fat cow. You two made a nice couple. Two losers. You better be divorced."

Don and Gillian walked away from me, back to the condo. I stared at the ocean for a while, but it didn't help.

It's always been this way. I'm weak and the rest of them, Dad and Don and Topper and Gillian, they torture me. All of my memories are like this— somebody telling me what to do, pointing a finger in my face, scolding me. Slapping my face.

Pop always said, 'You need discipline.' As if he ever had any. As if he ever obeyed a rule in his life, or took an order from anyone. Or any of the rest of them. Everyone did what they wanted. They made me join the Navy so they could brag about having a son in the service—'my son the Ensign,' the old man would introduce me at the Maplewood Country Club like I was a hero, his patriotic son, then he'd shoo me away so he could drink scotch and make deals with his cronies. When I went AWOL in Manila and got a dishonorable discharge, Pop finally shut up about my naval career. He gave me money to go to school and told me to keep out of his sight. That was fine with me. It wasn't my fault. The things that happened to me could have happened to anyone.

All of this has gotten me over-excited. I have high blood pressure. One hundred eighty-five over ninety-five this morning. I take vasodilators and calcium-channel blockers, renin inhibitors and endothelin-receptor antagonists, though when my doctor explained this family of drugs I wasn't attentive and so I don't understand what they do. I also take Parnate, and Nardil to inhibit serotonin uptake. That's what it says in the pamphlet. I like the idea of these little guards arresting my endorphins and keeping me on track. None of these drugs would be necessary if they would leave me alone.

I wish I had my fishing pole. I enjoy fishing. Hooking something. The battle with the invisible fish. The surprise when the fish breaks the surface of the water. You don't know what you've got, it might be a trout or a grouper, or a weed, or a rusted beer can. Even catching a beer can is better than being married, having to report to your wife like a little boy. It's better to be on your own, to do what you feel like doing. That's what I've been trying to do my whole life—be who I am. Somebody told me once that every person is a world; our minds are populated with memories and ideas and images that make us who we are. Don and the rest don't understand this fact; they don't know what I really am.

The invisible fish. That's who I am—the sleek invisible fish gliding through the immense ocean, never stopping, too smart for the hook or the net, a silvery diamond when I jump into the light. The ocean is full of us, the ones who can't be caught, beautiful ones, invisible in the deep black Gulf.

167

Mom will be awake by now. She'll have a headache and be on edge until cocktails. Then we'll start arguing about dinner. Of course we'll go out; nobody cooks. Seafood or Chinese. Mom doesn't eat much but likes to dress up and drink in a nice place.

I don't deserve what happened. I shouldn't have hit my wife—that was wrong. But I went to confession. The priest gave me ten Our Fathers and an Act of Contrition. I forgot to say them. It doesn't matter. It's forgiven now, it's all forgiven.

Maybe the grouper are running. Stippled gray and black, beautiful fish that slide through the water like bullets. Thick as your arm, their eyes dull as you unset the hook and drop them in your bucket. They don't move while they drown in the air.

If I caught one Mom would be proud of me.

Something Happened

A couple of weeks before I left for Nicaragua for the final time, I went to the library downtown on Chestnut Street. There were some maps I wanted to look at and a video tape I'd read about, a *Frontline* episode, that I wanted to watch. I spent a couple of hours in the warm building, avoiding the homeless men and women who slept on the big worn-out tables, then went back through icy winds to my apartment. I made a can of soup and a sandwich, some coffee with a little rum. After I finished eating I spent a couple of hours studying Spanish—I was getting better, but still didn't have enough words. I read over some old issues of *Barricada* and poems by Neruda. I loved the language, the soft feeling of the vowels, words like *cielo* and *azul* that were pretty in the mouth. My hunger for the words, for the light and sounds and smell of Nicaragua was an ache in my heart. I went to my old phonograph and played my worn out records of Victor Jara and Violetta Parra and Silvio Rodrìguez. If I could have stood aside or above myself for a moment I might have been embarrassed by my behavior. I knew better.

Late at night I pulled the cassette out of my rucksack. The video was brand-new. I don't like movies of any sort, or television, or anything on film, but I needed as much information as I could gather. I had the kind of knowledge that comes from books, but since I was afraid of what might happen to me, since I knew what might happen to me, I wanted to be as prepared as I could. The film might help.

I popped the cassette into a player that I'd borrowed from my brother. A lot of images, talk; strident narration by a famous American journalist. Then came the part I'd heard about, old footage, the Kid.

I want to write this out to help me remember. I didn't know it at the time, but those five minutes of *Frontline* were prophetic—they came to symbolize what happened. What happened to me, to my friend Bill, to all of us.

The year of the film is 1934. A young Marine is smoking a cigarette and staring away from the camera. The interviewer is a voice off screen. His questions are matter-a-fact, bored. The Marine has short blond hair and looks weary. His fatigues are muddy; so are his face and hands. I was paying close attention, absorbing every detail. I know how to be patient. The boy—he looks maybe eighteen—has an accent that suggests the upper Midwest, one of those counties that is filled with corn and soybeans throughout the summer and snow all through the winter. I'm thinking Minnesota, the Dakotas, a town whose flatness is broken by the steeple of the Methodist Church and the tower of the grain silo. I've been to these places.

As the film rolls, I'm filling in the blanks. I'm sure the Marine is devout, hard-working. Like my family, going into the military was expected. I'd guess both his father and grandfather served in the military—his father in Cuba or the Philippines. Maybe his grandfather fought in Mexico, the great war of Manifest Destiny, charging Mexican boys, peasants, in Monterrey or Chapultepec. Someplace foreign and hot, someplace that made the young Marine's grandfather dream of cool autumn nights at a fishing camp on Lake Clarke—someplace not in the terrible desert where the dry air sucks the tears from your eyes.

The young Marine who speaks to the journalist has a flat twangy tone, just like my folks, the ones from Jersey, they all drop their 'h's' and cut their vowels in half. I never gave any thought to how people speak until I started to learn Spanish and went to different countries—places I'd only dreamed of seeing. You learn to listen carefully.

Looking at the film, my first thought is, no emotion, the kid's numb, but then I understand, he's holding back. And something else I know, from my own father and uncles, from myself too, an odd thought, against everything we are told: the kid wasn't fighting for his country; he wouldn't have dreamed of fighting for his country. Seems strange when you put it that way, but I know that it's true.

"Can you tell me about the ambush?" an off-screen voice asks.

The boy—as I look at him on the film he grows younger, and if I close my eyes I remember boys with whom I fought, half a century later—starts slowly, no feeling.

"Sergeant sent me and Chilly and Scab to the ditches. He said look out, the bandits are hidden somewhere near. You gotta go real slow and find them. Just see how many, draw fire if you have to but stay in the bush, low down, see," the boy now points behind him, and I realize that he is sitting on the edge of an *acecia*, right where the firefight took place. The Marine points with a dirty finger back toward the sluggish brown water and the thick strands of what looks like salt cedar and sumac. He looks back toward the camera for just a second, then he looks away; he shakes a cigarette out of his pack and, in an instant, a hand reaches into the frame of the film holding a wooden match to light it.

"Go on son."

"We didn't like it. Boys been getting shot up all month. Them bandits hide in ditches and woods and shoot us then pick up a hoe and start working them little bean patches they got. Straw hats and like these pajamas they wear, can't tell who's what. But Sergeant don't like no sass and me and Chilly said okay and picked our buddy Scabby to go with us."

"Scabby?"

"On account of his face being all red. It's Milton. Was."

"Then what happened?"

The Marine gestured with his head. The camera panned away from him. There were two covered bodies on the ground no more than ten feet away. I was startled. Why were the bodies still there? The camera crew and the voice weren't attached to this kid's unit—it wasn't Vietnam. Somebody had held the bodies back to set the scene for the interview. I could see that it was hot. The smell of his buddies must have contributed to the young Marine's ashen look. He was chain-smoking to cut the stench.

"We humped down this way from up there"—none of this was very clear, but I knew what the Marine meant. When somebody might shoot at you it's hard to say where you are exactly. You're just in yourself.

"We crept close to the ground at first, spread out, real quiet, listening. Weren't no sounds but the bugs and birds squawking, the water brushing the bank below us. Half-hour passed and we sort of relaxed." The kid looks down and is silent, then looks right at the camera, defiant, pissed off.

"So?" The voice is bored.

"So we sat together and had a smoke. Nothing was doing and we decided to go back. Hell, can't nobody blame us. Couldn't see a thing, no bandits around that we could see. You know you can smell 'em when they're close by"—he scowls—"they stink with sweat."

Smoke blows into the picture from somewhere. Everyone is puffing away; I would have lit up myself, if I still smoked. The camera wobbles for just a second. It's not on a tripod. There are voices off screen; a tight laugh. The young Marine looks away to the side and spits. Looks back and whispers 'sorry' to no one in particular.

I look at my watch. Three minutes have passed since I pushed the cassette into the machine. I say, aloud, 'Holy shit' meaning, I guess, how long this seems, or, maybe, how short. For ten years after I returned home from the war I refused to read about war at all, or to watch shows about it on television, or to go any of the dozens of movies that were made to lament it, or celebrate it, or give those who never tasted it a thrill. All that Rambo bullshit Americans love. My non-vet buddies thought I should lighten up, but I couldn't—why should I? I liked war well enough when I was a kid. But when I was twenty and somebody shot at me for the first time, all bets were off. Some guys I knew got off on the adrenaline, the rush of combat. It never appealed to me. But here I was, plugged into this little Marine's story, riveted, just because it was real. And I thought that if the kid hadn't got killed in Nicaragua that year or the next, or in the Pacific in '43, because I'm guessing he'd volunteer, then today he's in his seventies and still thinking about that day sitting by the irrigation ditch with Chilly and Scabs. I have my own pictures that I would like to forget but can't and, I suppose, never will. You never can forget the things you want to forget, just everything that you should remember. This is a hard truth that I've come around to: memory is treacherous.

Anyway, the kid looks at the camera again, and shrugs, and then the screen goes black. There is a short pause, and there he is again, calmer, and ready to talk. Now his tone is flat and he looks right at me.

"We turned back and went a couple of clicks toward the platoon when they come out of nowhere and hit us. Chilly fell right down in front of me before I heard the shots. I felt the rounds go over my head and jumped down toward the ditch. Scabs yelled 'I'm hit,' and I rolled back toward him. Poppoppop everywhere. Chilly wasn't moving. I grabbed Scabs and pulled hard. He said some words to me, basically, leave me be. But I pulled on him some more and we rolled to get away and still the bullets were hitting around us, I got hit in my foot, just a dinger, and I looked around but couldn't see no bandits. And no one of us had even fired his weapon, which I know was wrong. But we rolled down toward the ditch and the water 'cause I had this idea we'd be okay if we got to it. And we splashed in and then, I don't know, I held onto my buddy then he was gone. I don't know. I don't know what happened. They got us. We were sitting ducks and they killed them two and now I got to figure out what I could of done."

'I got to figure out what I could of done.' Hearing this makes me feel better.

The tape goes dark. I pour myself a drink.

I went to Nicaragua to do some good. I met a guy there, Bill Howell, whose death made it into the papers but not the TV. Bill was a friend, but he was more than that. I want to say that he was a saint, but nobody believes in sainthood anymore, so I'll just say he was a good man. That should be enough. Bill was killed a while back, murdered in a horrible way—butchered. There isn't much doubt who did it—not who, like a guy's name, but what group, which army. When I heard about Bill's murder I wasn't surprised but I was angry. Part of how I felt had to do with everything else that happened to me in Nicaragua, but my rage went deeper. I think I went a little crazy.

The trouble with places like Vietnam and Nicaragua—there will always be such places—is that the truth slips away. Years later, when people sit around in bars in Miami and Washington and Managua, trading stories about life in Nicaragua during the Revolution and the war, no one can seem to agree on anything. Lying is a part of the problem; everyone does it. The governments of all the countries involved, the journalists who pretended to report what they saw—most of them never saw anything—the aid workers who lie to elicit sympathy for their particular cause, and all the good people who were there to help—they lie too, out of shame for how little they lost when others lost so much, or out of vanity, or because they just forgot. Forgetting is so easy. Here at home the air seems like a fog of forgetting, to breath it is to choke on things too terrible to remember.

In the North, up on the Honduran border, where Bill lived and died, truth was non-existent. In the jungle that surrounded the Rio Coco, in the tiny pueblos that cling to the hillsides, there was only power. The state of nature that fools yearn for, where everyone is free to do what he wants, where all the rules are suspended. More and more of us seem to be drawn to this vision, this idea of ending the rules. I guess we think we'll always be on the winning side.

My friend Bill Howell went there to help. He worked to bring electric light to a tiny town that otherwise sank into oblivion each night. He lived alone, not far from the people he served. One night, they killed him. They came across the river and did what they wanted. One night they wanted to kill the thin man from the United States who was probably a communist. And they did.

More than a year ago, during my second stint in Nicaragua, working up in the north in the "special zone"—the war zone, where the *contras* operated freely—I was bushwhacking out of a tiny pueblo north of Ocotal. There are trails in that part of the country, but everyone knew that if you walked them you might meet up with the *contras* and that if you did they would probably shoot you. But someone in Managua had told me that five or six kilometers outside of Ocotal, in the dense forest that covered the mountains, some gringo naturalist had spotted an ivory-billed woodpecker. The ivory-bill is officially extinct—the last bird was supposedly seen in Cuba a decade ago—but there was this buzz that the ivory bill was nesting near the Rio Coco as the river wound its way south from the Honduran border into Nuevo Segovia. I wasn't a naturalist, but I was trying out optimism, so the idea of seeing a quetzal, or a trogon, or, best of all, the ivory bill was irresistible. The thought that something beautiful and presumed dead was alive in the middle of a war gave me a rush. So there I was, I can recall the whole thing vividly, walking through the heavy forest, looking for a bird that I was pretty sure I'd never find, hoping not to see any bad guys.

I humped the bush for three or four hours without seeing a thing except a javalina and a couple of hundred parrots. Then, in the distance, I heard a high-pitched screeching. I began to creep through the underbrush as quietly as I could, on edge, hoping I wasn't going to defy the odds and run into a *contra* patrol. Through a break in the trees, I saw a brown-skinned fellow— he looked American—who was so thin that his bones seemed to jump out of his skin. This apparition was using a propane torch to spot weld an electric generator. It was Bill Howell. I walked up on him. When I got close he jumped and turned off the torch.

"Scared the shit outta me."

"Likewise."

"What are you doing here?"

"You wouldn't believe me if I told you. And you?"

"Try me. I live here. I work here."

"You live here? This isn't anywhere. You mean you live in Quilalí?"

"Nope, my house is right through that clearing. I don't like living in town. I'm a country boy."

"That's good. There's what, twelve people living in Quilalí?"

"More like twenty. Here I got peace and quiet. And now you tell me what you're doing here. I haven't seen an American in eight months."

"I'm looking for a bird."

"You've come to the right place. There's about a thousand birds right in this little patch of woods."

"An ivory bill woodpecker. Bet you haven't seen one of those. Not here or probably anywhere else."

"I wouldn't know. You an ornithologist? That'd be a first. Last poor gringo I saw was looking for oil."

"No man, I'm just a tourist. Been working in Ocotal. Wanted to look around some and thought I'd check out the rare wildlife."

"It's wild for sure." Bill grinned at me. He had sandy hair and thick glasses. The lines on his face were deepened by the dirt that covered him. "Anyway, I'm Bill Howell."

"Henry Lansdale. I gotta say you are a sight. I thought you were *contra* or a panther when I heard the screeching. What're you welding?"

"This here's a rack for bracing a rotor assembly for a micro-generator. I'm laying it up above that stream, see there," Bill points vaguely east with a lean muscled arm, "then I'm going to run some power cord to my shack and see if it'll light a bulb. If it works I'm going to pack it to Quilalí and light 'em up. That way the good folks can play dominoes after sundown. Go to the malls."

"Huh. And who's paying for the gear? This a government project?"

"No way. I don't deal with governments. My friends back home send the money and parts or else people carry stuff in for me or I just fabricate it out of junk. I don't even think anybody knows I'm here but my neighbors. And now you."

"I don't know anybody. Like I said, I'm a tourist. I've been helping out with a clinic in Ocotal. Semi-skilled labor."

"You know how to use tools?"

177

"Sure. I'm a mechanic, cars mostly, but I know how to fix most kinds of engines."

"So why aren't you doing that? Every truck and bus in the country is broken."

"Couldn't get a job. My Spanish is bad, plus I don't know anybody. I came here cold a year ago. So I've been picking up odd jobs, following leads from other internationalists."

"I hate that word. That 'internationalist' thing really burns me."

"Why's that?"

"Don't you get it? This isn't some cause. This is somebody's country. You think your neighborhood is 'international'? Of course not. So why turn the neighborhood of these good people into some kind of cause? Plus the word just brings down more shit on our neighbors—commies being supposedly enemies of the local."

"Yeah, well, it's just a word. And everything here is political."

"That's bullshit too. Who you been talking to? Tomas Borges? Nothing, my friend, is political."

"That's gonna surprise the hell out of the people getting shot by the *contras*."

Bill frowned and turned back to his welding. He ignored me for five minutes. I stood there, not feeling uncomfortable, just watching him work. He had a nice touch with metal; his welds were clean, no dirty joints. I could weld some, but I made a mess. Craftsmanship is something I admire. After finishing up a couple of braces Bill turned off his torch and smiled at me.

"Come on up to the house."

Bill lived in a tiny *casita*, maybe ten feet by fifteen, with a dirt floor and a couple of crude tables. There was a five-gallon plastic water jug on one table and burlap sacks of beans and corn. In the back corner he had built a stove out of an oil drum. His bed was the usual hammock; and there were a couple of wood chairs, a low table stacked with books, and tools stacked up against the wall.

The tools caught my eye right away. Everything in the room was sort of raggedy and patched together, but his tools were neat and clean, stacked up in plastic buckets and carefully built tool boxes.

"Nice Dewalt router you got here. Bet you don't use that much."

"Never. But you never know. I might start making furniture after we get some power going."

"So why're you so pissed off about politics and internationalists? What gives with that?"

"Because the people who talk like that don't do anything to help this country. And the people who do help don't have time for that bullshit. You've been to the clinic in Ocotal. Do the doctors argue politics? No way. They're too busy. I think the politics is a sideshow and, yeah, you're right, politics are killing these people which is why I don't deal with it."

"Fair enough. But what's going on here is political, like it or not."

"Henry, look, forget that. You're a mechanic, think about it. Nicaragua is an engineering problem. Once they can stand on their own they'll be all right. They won't need anybody. We're just pitching in for a little while till that happens. Just don't make things too complicated."

That was Bill. Keep things simple. The world is an errant machine, but fixable. We sat in the little house for most of the afternoon, talking. I hadn't done that in a long time—just talked to someone.

Bill was from Trout Run, a farming community in eastern Pennsylvania. Growing up, his neighbors were mostly Amish dairy farmers who plowed with horses, heated with wood. Bill's father was an old-fashioned Methodist who hated the modern world. Bill told me that even when he was a kid he loved to build things, and that school hadn't been much in the hilly outback of Trout Run—he'd literally attended a one-room schoolhouse—but he knew something about working hard and had taught himself enough math and science to win a scholarship to Worcester Polytech. By growing up isolated he had developed a thirst for the world. Some people stay put and remain content with the little they know; others can't settle down. I guess Bill and I had this in common. Being an only child on a farm in a small town gave him plenty of time to wonder about things, and it also gave him patience and compassion. Anyway, he had those qualities, however he'd come to them.

In his solitary shack, Bill filled notebooks with drawings and equations and weather reports and reflections—ideas born in a place as far from the murkiness of the world as you could get. He fasted, though he didn't call it that; he drank only water, slept a few hours a night, and embraced the poverty of the people around him. I couldn't tell if Bill was edging toward sainthood or just trying to fix what was broken around him. Because he and I were alike in a few superficial ways, I thought we must also be alike in the ways that counted the most. I was wrong about this. It's a mistake that I've made a few times in my life, seeing myself in others.

That afternoon I was kind of smitten by Bill. A funny way to put it, but I have to admit it's the right word. Bill was appealing, not charismatic, but solid in a way that I admired.

Like me, Bill had learned about Nicaragua by accident—from an article in the Williamsport newspaper written by someone who had visited the country. Operating in the methodical way he did, he went to the public library and read everything he could find on the country. He liked what he read and decided to visit, to see if he could do something tangible.

"I'm like my father," Bill told me. "We were isolated. No one ever said so, but we knew that our life was a throwback—my parents never had driver's licenses. We never had a phone, never paid taxes. We were off the grid, the way the hippies wanted to be, but we really were. But there's no beauty in poverty. The idea is to keep the dignity but to make life better. That's why I came to Nicaragua."

"But why here? I've been asking myself why I'm not back home doing this stuff. There are poor people at home too. Don't you wonder if we're missing something? I listen to my *compañeros* working at the clinic and honestly, aside from the Spanish, I don't have an idea what they're talking about. What are they dreaming about Bill?"

"That's the wrong question. It's way simpler. We're needed. If I go home I'll be making money, buying stuff, but I'd be redundant. You and I are nobodies back in the world, but here we make a difference."

"What if you get killed? The bad guys don't give a shit if you're essential or not. They might decide to shoot you *because* you're essential."

"No way. There's no percentage in the *contras* offing us. There would be a shit-storm if we turned up dead. What is it now, a hundred million, paying for this war—that's real money. No way this can go on for much longer. We can walk away from here in ten years and say that we changed the country, made a difference. What could be better than that?"

Nothing that I could think of. Trouble was, I wasn't sure what could be won. What exactly were we talking about? Would there be justice? And, if so, whose version?

"I think you're too ambitious Bill. Think of all the fuck-ups in the name of solidarity and brotherhood. Maybe Ortega isn't Pol Pot, but who is he? Do we know what we're doing here? And first off, get out of here. Come to Estelí. At least you won't be at ground zero."

"Nope. It's the people out here who need me. I'm maybe bringing lights to these *alcaldes*, fresh water, and irrigation if I can get the pumps. And I like being alone."

On it went. I wanted to save Bill, but didn't know how to do it. There's nothing worse than stomping on someone's ideals.

He'd say to me, after my lecture on being safe, "There's nothing but ideals. How do you think you got here? Your life was going nowhere, right, and you wanted to be doing something worthwhile. You've got to take some risks. Nobody can sit on the sidelines anymore."

"Risks, okay, but let's put that into perspective. You're not 'taking risks.' You're playing with doom. What's coming out of this?"

"Whatever we want."

As he said this, Bill looked at me in the way he did, with affection and sadness. I knew he thought I was decent but dishonest. I couldn't return his stare. And I couldn't shake the feeling that I'd known Bill before, that I'd always known him. I thought—and I pushed this out of my mind quickly— that I could see Bill dead.

"This isn't some Amish dairy farm. This is a death trip, like some nightmare you have over and over again. Whatever we want isn't even one of the options. It's whatever they want, up north there, across the river, or way up north, up where the shots are called. We're nothing here at all. Just the extras in some movie."

"I'm not Amish Henry. And I'm not foolish or sentimental either. I think you're striking a pose here. You've seen war and I haven't, but I've been here longer than you. Things are getting better."

On holy days, in the northern departments of Nicaragua, peasant farmers put down their crude tools and celebrate—Palm Sunday, Pentecost, the Assumption. In the tiny village of Ocotal, little more than a handful of shabby houses with outlying farms, every person who isn't too old gathers in the town center. Sugar candies are given to the children; the women talk and eat beans and tortillas; the men drink *chichi*, a cheap, intoxicating wine made from corn. Late in the afternoon, as weariness settles over the crowd, a tall, lanky young man with burnished brown skin rides into the town on a unicycle. He is juggling three rubber balls and wearing a red fright wig. The children and their parents perk up; the little ones squeal with delight. The man, called *Pulgarcito*—with great affection—is an American. He lives alone in a tiny *casita* a few kilometers north, right on the border with Honduras. The man smiles manically as he juggles; he yells out the names of the men and women he knows and mugs and waves and drops the balls. The balls scatter; the children pick them up and run to return them. The thin gringo laughs and musses the children's hair, tells them to keep the balls, asks them if they have been to church. After a short time he turns his little cycle around and rides back north, out of town. He would like to stay and drink and talk, but he is shy and afraid of not fitting in. He is afraid of crowds and of not having anything interesting to say. He is afraid of being alone and afraid of not being alone. He is afraid of a great many silly things that needn't concern him, but do. One thing he is not afraid of is dying.

And so that week before I went back to Nicaragua for the last time, sitting alone in my room or in the library, I thought about Bill.

What did he think about the night that they came for him? He must have been lying in his hammock, and if it were after dark he was probably asleep. He worked from sunrise until dusk; he ate simple meals, the meals of the *campasinos*. He slept deeply, alone, so far away from the world that he might have been on another planet.

I couldn't shake this image from his mind. Bill lying in his hammock, awake.

He heard their rough footsteps outside. The parrots that filled the trees squawked and flew off. He knew who it was. He might have prayed, but this seems unlikely. It wasn't that he didn't believe, but his faith was in the work he did with his hands, and not in anything as uncertain as God. They came for him. He walked outside—he wouldn't have cried out or resisted for there was no one in the world who could hear. They hit him and kicked him for a while, maybe until he was unconscious, and then cut his throat. To show the others what they thought of gringo engineers and doctors and teachers they hacked off his right hand. He had strong hands that had always known work. What better way to show that nothing was possible?

Later on I tried to think about what I was doing on the day and night of Bill's death. I was home in Philly. I talked to some people, looked in the *Inquirer*, and was eventually able to piece together my comings and goings. The truth is I wasn't doing much of anything. I probably worked, read a book, ate a meal, talked to friends, and went to bed. On that same day the President made a speech to supporters outlining for anyone who had been living on Mars the nature of the communist menace, praising those living under tyranny for their courage, and calling for continued support in the fight against evil. The stock market went up, then down, then closed one point higher than it had opened. Trading was probably brisk. The Phillies lost their spring training game to the Mets, 3-0. My mother wasn't sure, but she thought it was a nice day. The truth is I forget the day entirely, and when Bill was killed I was probably asleep.

I'm going back there, to the Northern provinces, to live where Bill lived, to do the work he did, though I know I won't do it as well. My motives aren't entirely clear, but clarity isn't always the most important thing. There are many things that I don't understand, but that too is unimportant.

But what I do know is that something happened, not just to Bill, but to all of us. Something that can never be undone. We let it happen, and now we're like the Kid in the newsreel, dazed and wondering how things went so wrong.

The Snowman

"The imagination, the one reality
In this imagined world."
Wallace Stevens

Lily loves winter days. The cold doesn't bother her, and she finds gray skies calming. When, like today, she is at home, she bakes bread and sips tea in front of the fireplace. Her daughter is with her, a calming presence filling the small rooms of the apartment. Lily has been alone long enough to become comfortable with the voices that fill her head. The words that she speaks to Katherine—that was the name she gave to her child—are gentle and concern the ordinary affairs of life.

Lily has given up trying to find full-time work. She hasn't the energy for it, and has settled into a routine of working a couple of days a week in a flower shop in the mall. She had been a teacher once, but since her divorce, as her hopes evaporated, what she thinks of as her public persona has weakened like the light on a January afternoon. The faith that sustains a teacher, belief in the future, in the reasonableness of things, has left her, and now she is finished with all of that—finished forever. Let the rest of them go on with their lives she thinks, I am content to be what I am.

Lily receives money each month from her ex-husband—not from him exactly, but from someone in his family. It isn't much, but it suffices, and she feels justified in taking it since he has taken everything from her. It is blood money. All money is blood money Lily thinks. Those who love it, who are seduced by it, are damned. Lily hates the little envelope that comes on the first of the month, with its violet handwriting, her name written in loopy letters, no return address, a check inside, never a note, never any words of condolence or sympathy, just money, a check signed by her husband's mother. You could almost feel the act of will it took for that woman to write a check; she loves money so, loves her houses, the piles of furniture, credenzas and sideboards stuffed to bursting with tattered tablecloths, torn sheets piled in the closets, threadbare towels, all passed through the family like precious gems—junk, but worshipped for their talismanic power to connect to the past, a sordid past of money grubbing and buying "the best," a favorite expression in that household, "we have the best," silver and place settings and cuts of meat and carpets, whatever it was achieved a hallowed status because it had touched their hands, hands soaked in blood as far as Lily is concerned. The father and mother passed greed to their children along with cold blue eyes and sandy hair. No pity in them, Lily thinks as she sits and sips chamomile tea in the silence of her apartment. All that she has left is crammed into a couple of rooms, the walls thin plasterboard, the ceiling stained brown from melting snow, the other tenants at work at the M&M factory or in the mall, the town an enclave of blue-collar futility surrounded by opulent suburbs, Tudor homes packed into *cul de sacs*, with nothing to distinguish Elm from Oak from Poplar except the landscaping, *no place* Lily says aloud, but this is home, and she will make the best of it.

Each morning Lily says, "I am recovering." It isn't clear what this means, but thinking it, saying it aloud, gives her a sense of purpose. I am a gentle person, Lily thinks, not worldly, not avaricious, not like the ones who push and shove in the shops, who blow their horns at me as I bike to work. I wish no one ill, and yet all I encounter outside of this room is anger. I'm in a hurry they say, what's wrong with you, *dense* someone called me, *stupid, clumsy*—my fingers don't work right, I'm distracted, no one stops to chat, even the blue-haired ladies from the Methodist Home rush around, finding fault, the roses are wilted, the tulips drooping. In the middle of winter flowers tire quickly, they bend their heads in the draft, the life in them is weakened by the dim sun. We all need to rest in these dark months, but no one lets us, the air reeks of weariness, working from dawn to nightfall, children forgetting their parents' faces, everyone worn out—and why?

Lily sips her tea and closes her eyes. She enjoys these moments, the memories they evoke. She has made one mistake in her life, only one, but sometimes a single error can be enough to unravel what has been otherwise so carefully woven—years of hope and calm happiness can disappear in an instant. Lily was singularly unprepared for the world's cruelty.

Lily thinks, as she always does, as she cannot help herself from doing, in a magical way, in the way of children who wish for things they cannot have— her thoughts a circle that turns on the axis of a few ideas day after day—*if only* things didn't happen so fast, *if only* you could grab onto the past and pull it back to you, cover yourself in those warm afternoons. If only I weren't swept into things I don't understand. If only I could control my thoughts. *If only*.

Oh Lily my boss says—fifty and unmarried, she wears make-up, never touches a flower in the shop, sits in her office with the books, on the phone— *oh Lily you're so naïve, so dreamy*. This and that in me need to be fixed, as if I were a broken-down car, all the things that were once good are tainted. Dress *sexier* Lily, you should lose weight Lily, you should use make-up, cut your hair Lily, you look so *frumpy*, that was the word Karen used, *dull, gray*, I'm a matron who sits and drinks tea with her cats—well, what of it?

Lily tries a prayer, or something like that—words projected out of herself, tossed into space like the flocks of hardy juncos who over-winter, flitting from the snow into the bare branches, words that mean nothing but carry a weight of feeling, of yearning. Lily knows that there's no point in praying. She had prayed fervently during the endless day that her baby was dying inside her—if God had wanted to do something that would have been the time. But He was otherwise occupied, Lily thinks, or as disinterested in me as I am in Him. But it feels good to leap out of her own mind. It is a relief to talk to someone else even if that someone isn't listening and doesn't care. Lily knows that life is made up of gestures, bows to convention, acting, reciting lines, playing parts. Alone, she needn't be anyone she isn't, but that doesn't make her loneliness any less of a burden.

And then Lily thinks—and it hurts to do so—*my darling girl*, rest quietly. I would have been a good mother. Katherine's gravestone, the flowers, fresh daises, the shade trees under lowering skies, I haven't gone in weeks, I am afraid to feel so empty. Does my husband feel the same way? Does he visit Katherine sometimes, or has he forgotten her as he has forgotten me?

Lily knows the answer. He has forgotten. Lily's brother has told her that some people can't feel. There's no pity in them, no compassion. Lily remembers that when her brother was in the war he would write long letters home about what he saw, about the cruelty of it, about how a few of the men seemed to enjoy the violence, and he wrote that he wouldn't let that happen to him. He said that he made himself feel, that he looked at things no one should see so he wouldn't stop feeling. But there was nothing he could do to stop from dying inside. He wrote that he "loved life more than ever," and he underlined the words *more than ever.* I didn't know what to write to him—Lily admits that she failed to understand what her brother had lived through. The normality of her life, its comfort, shamed her. I couldn't imagine what he was living through. I was worrying about algebra and the prom, about boys, and he was calling air strikes on villages. He told me later that he had thought about calling the bombs in on himself, but *he loved life more than ever.* "God help me Lily," he said, *"I want to live."*

Lily knows that the war took her brother away, but he had told her that *war* was just a word. Lily did not understand at first, but now she does.

Sitting in her chair, with the fire burning out, the dusk gathering on the runty hills of New Jersey, Lily naps and dreams of nothing at all, and when she wakes up she reflects on how it frightens her to think about her brother and that it is wrong to be afraid of someone you love. She tries to remember the happiness of growing up, the warm days that seemed to go on forever. She recites words aloud whose meaning is no longer clear to her: *And I would walk on those summer mornings along the shore, stroll onto the jetties and look at the crabs in the tide pools, shoo away the gulls, peek in the white buckets of the fisherman, the spray on my face, my feet warm in the sand or cold in the water—the water briny and the spume made my hair curly and my brother would tell me how pretty I looked with brown curls.* Now Lily's hair is thin and gray and lies on her shoulders like a worn cloak. She asks herself if this body could be the one she had on those summer mornings. Can this be me, Lily wonders, my legs knotted with veins, my knees aching, my stomach folded like an animal? Lily knows that the sadness of the body can be palpable, but mourning its aging is the worst sort of vanity. I am this person, she thinks, and nothing is as true as this.

And then, as the sun sets, or rather, as the light is blown away in the winter wind, Lily remembers her husband. When I met him he told me that I was pretty, Lily thinks, and he said I was interesting and smart. So much depends upon what you are told, what you want to hear from others. We sustain ourselves with so little. And she says aloud, as she does every day, *I don't hate him*, and she believes this to be true; indeed, believing in her own goodness is at the core of her life. She won't, or can't, hate a man who deserves her hatred. What better way to accept what has happened to you? What Lily believes is that two people who once lay together, who almost had a baby, who may have loved one another, that these two people can never feel hatred for each other. She knows this isn't true, but like the voice of her daughter, or the memory of her brother, Lily's handful of convictions is what keeps her alive. It has always been this way, she thinks, I have always believed in love and in forgiveness. Much of what we tell ourselves is untrue, but who is to say that truth is more important than illusions?

It's snowing harder. Lily loves the silence of the snow. The sky no longer exists. Lily thinks *I should go outside to feel the snow on my face*. When I was young and it would snow we went to the beach. There's no place better than the ocean in a snowstorm, the way the flakes whirl above the waves, and settle on the sand and in the rills of water that puddle on the edge of the world. We put on our heavy coats and Mom held our hands. It felt good to hold her hand through my mittens and walk the empty streets toward the monotonous rush and recession of the waves—the sound was muted by the snow, and there was no other sound. You never saw anyone; we had the world to ourselves. We would yell at the top of our lungs and run in circles until we were dizzy, and then my brother would collapse onto the wet sand and make a double angel, an angel of snow and sand, and I'd do the same, and then Mom would lie down with us and we would snuggle together, just we three in the silence. And then, since he knew I was afraid of how quiet it was, and how strange it seemed to be outside in an empty world, my brother would begin to sing a song that I loved, a song about favorite things, and I would laugh and we'd run into the waves, letting ourselves get wet so that when we went home we could say how cold we were and how good it was to be inside where it was warm and bright. And on those nights I would go to bed perfectly happy, in love with everything, in a world that I knew would be as bright as a diamond when I woke up.

Lily stands up. The cat jumps to the floor. You have to let it go.

She gets her coat. She thinks: my birthday is next week. My brother sent me the same book he sends every year—I have fourteen copies, one for every year since he left the Army. The same book of poems, with a different poem underlined each time, his little comments scrawled in the margins around the poem like bits of tinsel on a Christmas tree. This one is perfect for today, "The Snow Man," a little sad, she thinks, though I don't understand what the writer is saying, the nothing at the end seems hopeless to me, but my brother underlined the word three times and wrote "yes" with exclamation points, and jotted in the margin "this is about us!" I don't see how. Snowmen melt. Leaves blow in the November wind. The oaks in New Jersey are bare by Thanksgiving, a few sycamores keep their leaves until Christmas, and the sky is the backdrop for the empty trees, and then the snow makes the land fresh, if only for a few days, then it melts and freezes over, the mud hard as rock, the roads edged with salt, the snow banks black with it.

The listener is me, I can see that, *nothing myself*, and I suppose that's how my brother sees himself, as a silent witness, the words *misery* and *bare* and *nothing, nothing, nothing* seem hopeless. He wrote in the margin, "winter is our time Lil, remember the ocean?" And Lily thinks—*Yes, I remember*. She says, aloud—I love these poems. It's odd and funny to receive the same book every year. Every year it means something different to me, the poems speak to me in a different way. In January when I open the thick envelope, knowing what is inside, I feel excited, as if I were seeing the book for the first time—my brother told me that we never go to the shelf and take down a book to reread it. Only a fresh copy opens our eyes to what the poet is telling us. *The nothing that is*, the nothing that is—making *nothing* into something rich and important, as if there were a shadow in the empty space that surrounds the listener, and the shadow could be filled in with whatever we wish, the face of a loved one or a memory. I am not afraid of nothing. Of emptiness. But I could not say that I am afraid of nothing, because there are many things to be frightened of. But to stand outside in the snow and feel the quiet is comforting. To stand alone and think about nothing. To stand alone in the cold a long time, until I can no longer think of any misery. Until there is no sound, the wind ceases, to listen to the nothing that fills this world.

Lily goes to the window. After a little while she decides to go outside. She leaves her coat on the chair. The cat jumps up onto the coat and settles in. Lily smiles at her cat and thinks how peaceful it will be to walk in the wind and to see gray snow silently covering the earth.

Lily is used to the cold, to the nothing that is, to the black night.

Afterword

I owe a great debt to my first readers for encouragement and support. Brigid Ovitt, Joan Marie Hart, Reginald Fitz, David Gutierrez, Steve Allen and Carlton Cuse were kind enough to find some value in these stories. My other first reader and dearest friend, David F. Noble, passed away in 2010 but spent thirty years listening to me talk about writing and many other things. Charlie Wendell provided me with a lift when I needed it most. My daughter Alexis is always there to talk to me about books and politics and life. My colleague, good buddy, fellow writer and bibliophile Peter Nash was kind enough to go over each of these stories and to make many helpful suggestions; without his aid there would be no book. My oldest friend, Michael Keith, is the effective midwife of this volume; I can't thank him enough for his friendship and support. To the good people at Blue Mustang Press I can only express my gratitude for their support of my writing. In the current climate of publishing, BMP is unique in its quiet professionalism.

Though these stories were written over a relatively short period of time, they hope to record something of four decades of American life as experienced by ordinary people.

The book that Lily holds in the final story is of course *Harmonium* by

Wallace Stevens.

No one is to blame for the infelicities that remain in this work. In the end, one follows one's own tastes and inclinations against the best advice of those who know better.

My family has been patient with me, and it is for them that I write—how better to know one another than through stories? Brigid, Dorothy, and Ada, Alexis, Mike and Sally Ovitt, Patricia Layton, Dorothy Demmel, Fred and Joan Hart—my extended Florida and New Mexico families—many thanks.

www.ingramcontent.com/pod-product-compliance
Lightning Source LLC
Chambersburg PA
CBHW020435180626
46812CB00003B/1247